Game On

Vivien Brock

It feels like the time slows down as I meet Nick's gaze. He doesn't look away and the glimpse in his eyes scares me and in the end, I'm the one who budges.

My eyes trail down his body as I breathe heavily, waiting for his first move.

The veins on his throat and neck are clearly visible and his hands are clenched into fists.

"You shouldn't have punched me, Alex", he says after countless of seconds in silence. I lower my lashes, look down at my feet, and bite my lip.

"I'm sorry...?" I whisper, but it comes out like a question and I glance up at him, starting to twinning my hair between my index- and middle finger.

"Sorry doesn't cut it this time", he tells me in an almost as quiet voice as me but the coldness in his tone scares me and as he takes a step towards me, a shiver runs down my spine and I take a step back.

"Then what can I do?" I try to plead without sounding too desperate, but all I get is a headshake.

"Nothing. That's how much you can do."

I open my mouth to literally beg him not to hurt me, but the words get stuck in my throat and I can't seem to utter them.

That's what he wants.

He wants me to beg him for mercy, he wants to feel like he's in total control and most important of it all; He wants to see with his own eyes that he's broken me.

GAME ON

I can't let that happen.

When Zeke left with Vince and Patricia, they slammed the door shut but they didn't lock it.

If I manage to get through the door I'll get a minimal chance of getting away. I can already tell for sure that the odds won't be in my favor, but it would postpone my punishment. And probably make it worse too, but I got to do this.

I can't just let Nick control me like a puppet.

"What will you do to me?" I ask Nick to buy time.

"You'll see", he sneers, "but firstly, do you got any phobias?"

My eyes widen slightly as I figure out his plan. Using my phobias against me. That's just pure evil and heartless. Only a monster would do that and that's just another proof of Nick's true nature.

I shake my head at his question.

"No, I don't. Except for one, and it's to be stuck with you forever."

He laughs dryly, the sound escaping his throat sounding more wicked and evil than if it would've come from the devil himself.

"Too bad you already have to face that fear and you better start enjoying it."

I pretend to gag at his words, realizing my mistake moments after as I see the anger flashing in his eyes.

"That's it. You've gotten too many chances. I didn't want it to come to this but the other guys are right. I've been too gentle with you but that's gonna change now with starting from your punishment. If you don't have any real phobia, I'll give you one."

With that, he throws himself at me and I move in the last second and sprint towards the door.

My hand reaches the handle and I'm just about to pull it down when I feel Nick taking a hold onto my hips, digging his fingers into the bone and causing me to whimper in pain.

I try to punch him and to kick him, I even try to bite him, but nothing works and I am grasping in the air for something to grab on to.

"Let me go!" I yell, not caring about the pointlessness in the action. Once the panic takes over, you don't control your actions like before.

"I hate you", tears of anger falls down my cheeks, "I hate you so much. You're a monster and I will never love you. Ever."

At the last words, I think I pushed too far because suddenly, I'm thrown against the wall and knock my head and back onto the hard concrete.

I groan in pain but before I manage to get up on my own, Nick takes a firm hold onto my upper arm and practically drags me into the bathroom.

My fear gets mixed with confusion as I see Nick tap up water in the sink and put the plug on. I try to wiggle out of the grip, bit it's in vain. Nick is too strong.

The grip is hurting me and I'm sure that it will leave bruises but that's the least of my worries right now.

The water fills the sink to the top and Nick smirks at me and I'm sure that I'm looking like a frightened deer. With his free hand, he takes a strong hold onto my hair and I scream in pain, but it ends up being muffled by the water I'm pressed into.

I start to panic even more as my lungs fills with water and I'm struggling to get over the surface with my hands - without succeeding.

GAME ON

I scream in the water for Nick to let me go, bubbles filled with air forming by my lips and floating to the surface.

Just as I start to feel light headed, I'm suddenly roughly pulled up and I immediately gasp for air.

"What do you think of your punishment?" Nick smirks, "I figured I didn't want to hurt the pretty face of yours."

He doesn't even give me time to reply before I'm pressed into the water again, but this time I manage to take a deep breath right before I hit the water, which is freezing cold for the record.

I hope that Nick will pull me back up to the surface soon enough before I run out of air, but I'm not that lucky. It seems like he knows exactly when the lack of oxygen is enough for me to pass out because it's not until then he pull me back up again. I gasp for air once again before getting my head pressed down - again. I don't even have time to take a full deep breath, but I am cut off halfway and swallow some of the water instead.

My lungs are screaming for air, my chest hurting, but Nick keeps going on.

And on... and on.

He continues with the procedure; pulling me down until my head is about to explode due to lack of oxygen, then pulling me up long enough for me to inhale quickly before pressing me down again.

Saying that I've got panic is an understatement.

I want to stay strong but as I'm in the water, helpless, it's hard.

I panic because every time I'm under the surface, I'm not pulled back up until right before I'm about to black out.

No matter how much I try not to, I'm fighting with my arms in vain because my brain tells me to.

Even though it's the last thing I want to do, I find myself begging Nick to stop.

He doesn't listen.

Nick's POV:

I ignore her pleadings and shove her back under the surface. Truth to be told, I'm not regretting what I'm doing.

This way, I won't hurt her that much physically but a lot more mentally. Physically, she'll be recovered in a matter of minutes but mentally on the other hand... it will leave her invisible scars.

If the only way to get her to listen to me is by scaring her, I'll do it.

All I want is for her to stay with me.

What's mine will stay mine.

What belongs to me will stay with me unless I say otherwise, which I don't do in this case.

Alex's mine and I want her to stay, therefore she will. No matter if she wants it or not.

A smirk is tugging at the corner of my lips as I see her futile attempt of getting out of the water and I wait for the right time, right before she'll pass out because of lack of oxygen, and pull her up.

Her eyes show fear as she looks at me with tears in her eyes and trembling lips. My smirk grows as she opens her mouth to beg me once more, and I shove her back in.

GAME ON

I continue with the action for countless of minutes until Alex's pointless attempts of getting free are long gone and she's given up and just sobs the short time she gets over the surface.

Her pitch black hair hangs in stripes around her cute face and I smile at her as she looks at me, completely terrified.

"You've learned your lesson?" I ask her as I'm towering over her.

Alex's POV:

I flinch back as he asks me the question and moves closer.

My shirt is soaking wet and my whole body is trembling, but not only by the cold.

When I stared into his eyes in the bedroom, right after when the other guys walked out, I thought that I could take the punishment, even though I was scared.

I was wrong.

If I would have gotten the chance to chose between the punishment I got, and being punched and kicked, I would have chosen the other alternative without any doubt.

I thought I was strong, but it seems like I've broke because of some water.

Only glancing at the water makes me shiver.

Never have I been so scared as I've been the last... countless of minutes that passed as I was slowly tortured in the water.

I knew he wouldn't kill me but that didn't stop the panic from rising inside of me.

It's an instinct. If you can't breathe, you'll fight for your life after the air you are in desperate need of.

It doesn't matter if you know that it will be fine moments after because the panic won't leave, and honestly, I don't think I'll ever forget the fear of being trapped under the icing cold water.

When Nick told me that he would give me a phobia since I didn't really have one, I thought he wouldn't succeed.

I wish I was right but sadly, I'm not.

I think I'm in shock because I barely notice and even less care when Nick picks me up and walk out of the bathroom and placing me on the bed.

He takes off his own shirt, which has gotten wet too, and slip under the covers with me, pulling my cold and tense body into his chest.

I can feel him stiffen behind me as he notice my cold shirt and he moves his hand to the hem of my shirt and starts tugging at it.

It's not until then I seem to care or show any emotions at all, but my hand immediately snaps to his and pulls down my shirt.

"C'mon, gorgeous..." he coos, "you're cold and you're in shock. It's not a good combination. You got to get the shirt off of you."

I don't reply and truth to be told, I barely hear him either. It's like I'm a mile away. His voice is just a sound in the background but I can't make out what he's saying and I can't concentrate on anything at all.

I'm just staring right in front of me, my body and mind absent.

It almost feels like a dream, unreal.

GAME ON

I can't take in what is happening, the only thing I can make out is the heat that is radiating off of Nick's hot body to my cold and still, thanks to the shirt, wet one.

Everything else is a blur.

Contents

Chapter 1: Rumour

I look at myself in the mirror that's hanging over the sink in my own bathroom. My black hair, dyed, is hanging in stripes around my heart-shaped face and with a sigh, I quickly take off my pyjamas, jump in the shower and shampoo my hair. The hot water is a welcoming escape from reality, if so just for a few minutes until I unwillingly step out of the shower and get dressed in a pair of dark, trashed jeans and a simple black tank top. Because it's winter and chilly outside, I also put on my black hoodie with the text "Leave me alone" standing in a big font at the back.

Don't get me wrong, I am not one of these socially awkward people who hates everybody, I just like the hood, and I am not one of this rich kids so I don't really own many clothes either.

As I put on my makeup, mostly eyeliner and red lipstick, Cuffy comes in and moan.

Cuffy is my "family's" cat and he is truly adorable with his brown fur with splashes of white.

I live in a foster care, my parents left me for adoption as soon as I was born and since then I've been moving back and forth over the country but I haven't found a place I can call home, not yet. But I don't really care. I am one of this easygoing people and I never dwell in the past.

I might have a different style, some people would call me for an emo but I honestly don't care what they think. I'm not one of the most popular girls in the school, but I'm not disliked either. I get along with everyone and got a bunch of really good friends. Especially Lindsey, who is my BFF.

As I am done with my makeup, I pick Cuffy up and cuddle with him for a few seconds before I peck him on his little cute head and run down to the kitchen where Carol, my guardian, stands by the counter with a pile of waffles by her one side and a waffle maker by her other.

"Mmm, smells good", I say as I sit down at the table and take a plate and fill it with waffles and maple syrup. She smiles at me in response. I really like Carol and her husband Brian, and their ten years old daughter, Lottie, is just adorable! Maybe I finally can settle down here? They are really nice, but I don't want to rush anything so I will just wait and see if my thoughts and feelings changes or not.

As I am done with the breakfast I put the plate in the sink and grab my white and black striped backpack and head towards school. Normally I would walk the twenty minutes it takes to get there, but the weather is really windy and it's snowing so I have decided to take the bus but as I walk to the bus stop, a blue car slows down and someone wind down the window, revealing a guy with untidy, brown hair and a nice smile.

"Hey, Alex", he says and I smile in response at my friend Peter.

"Want a ride to school?" he asks and I jump into the back. The driver is a blonde girl named Patricia, another one of my friends and Peter's girlfriend.

"I didn't know you ever let a girl drive your car", I tease Peter as I am safe from the cold, thankfully sitting inside the warm car.

"Usually, I wouldn't but I lost a bet and now I have to let her drive in my car to the school the rest of the week", he says with a sad tone. I chuckle and look out at the white street we pass and a few minutes later, we are parked at the school's parking lot and I step out in the icing cold winter and hurry inside the school building to my locker.

My first class is history, and I take my book and quickly walk to the right classroom where I sink down in a chair in the back and pull out my sketch pad. The teacher walks in and I continue on a painting of a werewolf I started with a few days ago. I don't know why, but I find it very relaxing to paint and it's a nice escape. If I only could put in my earplugs too, but I know that wouldn't go by unnoticed by my teacher who now has started calling up our names.

After the class I have a quick chat with Lindsey, who is hyper and glad as always with her curly red hair bouncing around her as she jumps up and down, telling me the latest gossip she just found out about. Mostly, like this time, I don't care about the gossip and Lindsey knows it, but that doesn't stop her from telling me everything anyways. Right now, her eyes are wide and I just hear her voice in the background. I got this great ability to shut out the rest of the world, which is very helpful at some times.

"Hello?", I hear her say as if she's far away. She waves with a manicured hand in front of me and I return to reality and look at her.

"Sorry, what did you say?" I ask her with a small smile.

She pouts at me. "You didn't listen at all!"

I apologize again and she gives me a glare before her mood changes back to cheery again and this time, I listen to what she has to say.

"There is this rumour that..." she lowers her voice and moves closer to me, "that we are going to be attacked today", she whispers.

I look at her serious face and break out into a laugh. "Where did you hear that?" I say in-between my laughs and she looks at me angrily.

"Stop it! It's not funny, I'm serious! Someone told me that she heard from a safe source that our school is going to be attacked, today. Apparently, the office got a letter or something telling them to look up and to be expecting guests today, and the principal decided to keep it a secret!"

I look at her with a confused face, my eyebrows furrowed. "Hey, Lindsey look", I say as I try not to smile, "someone probably just made this up, and even if it would be true, I'm sure its just a joke. Relax, nothing is going to happen."

She looks at me, truly worried. "B-but.."

I cut her off. "Nothing is going to happen, if the principal would've thought it was true, he would've told us by now", I say and flash her a reassuring smile before walking to my next class, mathematics.

Ugh.

After the painfully long lesson of mat torture, it's finally lunch and I head to the cafeteria and sit down with Lindsey, Patricia and Peter.

"Hey, guys", I say in a cheery voice as I put down my tray on the round table. They all welcome me with big smiles, except for Lindsey who looks at nothing particular with an absent face.

"Still worried about the threat, huh?" I ask her and she slips back to reality.

"What? Oh... yeah, I mean, no one seems to take any notice. What if it's true?"

Peter chuckles. "And what if it isn't?"

Lindsey sticks out her tongue at him. "Traitor. I thought you were on my side on this."

Peter holds up his hands in defense. "Hey, I'm just looking over the alternatives, and still, I think you got Patricia on your side."

I turn to Patricia who looks down into her lettuce. "You believe it?" I ask, slightly shocked.

"Well, I didn't say that", Patricia says with blushed cheeks, "but I don't think it's impossible. I mean, maybe it's true, maybe it's not. I just don't think we should wipe it away as nothing." She shrugs and ends the conversation, causing a tense silence to fall over the table.

Luckily for us, another tray is suddenly put down beside me at the table and Parker, one of the friendly guys on the football team, sits down.

Immediately, he starts talking about football with Peter and before we know it, everything has gotten back to normal.

"Anybody who knows what we're supposed to do in P.E.?" Patricia asks when we walk to our lockers. We all shake our heads.

The lunch break is over soon and we're just going to get our jackets before heading to the gym, which is in another building.

We soon step outside the main school building and luckily the snowing has ended, but I grab Lindsey by her arm, just in case if I would fall.

The walk to the gym only takes two minutes and we say bye to Peter and Parker as we walk into the girls locker room. Just as I have taken off my jacket, a scream fills the air and everyone stops in their motions.

"What was that?" a girl named Yasmine asks and suddenly more shrieks are heard and I follow Patricia as she runs out of the changing room. We open the entrance door and I have to put my hand in front of my mouth to prevent myself from letting a scream escape my throat. Patricia on the other hand, can't prevent herself and her loud voice hurts my eardrums but there is no time to bother about that. Patricia and I exchange a quick look, filled with fear and panic, and then we close the door leading outside. I turn the lock as well, making sure that no one will be able to step in or out.

"RUN! THEY HAVE GUNS. WE'RE UNDER ATTACK!" Patricia screams while she runs back to the changing room, repeating her words over and over again. Peter rushes out from the guys changing room and makes his way towards me. In a matter of seconds, the corridor is filled with panicking students who tries to push me away in order to reach and open the door.

"NO!" I scream. "YOU CAN'T TAKE THIS WAY OUT. DIDN'T YOU HEAR HER? THEY HAVE GUNS. GO BACK!" I shout at the top of my lungs but my words drown in all the other screams but Peter, out of all people, has heard me. He manages to place himself beside me and shout with an even louder voice than me;

"MOVE BACK OR ELSE YOU'LL GET SHOT. IDIOTS, MOVE BACK!" He catches their attention and suddenly, everyone turns around and start to move back instead, pushing and elbowing each other in their desperate fight to get back into the changing rooms.

I look out of the window and see a few dark figures approach, everyone with guns in their hands. I realize, that it's just a matter of seconds before they will be here. A movement by one of the dark-clothed people catches my attention. He, judging by the figure, is raising his hand, the one holding the gun, and I realize what he's about to do.

A wave of panic washes over me and I shout, with fear trembling in my voice; "EVERYONE GET DOWN!" Somehow, my voice reaches out and all students fall down to the ground as if on cue and the sound of shattering glass fills the panicked air. After that, everyone becomes more freaked out and quickly get up from the ground to continue their elbowing towards the changing rooms that one by one is getting locked by frightened students who are willing to leave some of their friends left out here in the corridor in order to, hopefully, save themselves.

I let out a gasp as someone pushes me hard on my side, causing me to fall down to the ground.

As I'm lying on the cold floor, I catch my breath and groan as I force myself to look up. Peter is now gone, and I hear a door slam shut and realize that I am the only one left in the entrance hall. I quickly get up, ignoring the pain in my side where I got elbowed by a panicking student. I don't know who did it, but I can't blame them either. My heart is pounding hard and fast in my chest and I make a quick decision as I take a look behind me at the intruders who now are beating and kicking at the door, trying to get in. I know it's just a matter of time before they succeed, and I also know that all changing room are locked for sure by now.

I meet the gaze of one of the intruders, my icy blue eyes locking with a pair of dark ones that almost seems to be black. Fear shoots through my body and I break the contact and turn around, opening the door leading into the gym and quickly closing it behind me. I rush to the small room where the equipment is held, and I slid down behind a gymnastic plinth and a bunch of thick, grey rugs. How come I am the only one here? I mean, wouldn't it be more students here? Or did everyone get into the changing rooms in time before they were all locked up? I hear the sound of glass breaking and realize why I am alone here. The glass doors into the gym, it's so easy to break through them, but the changing room doors, on the other hand, doesn't have any windows and you need a key to get into them. At least it's safer to be in a changing room than to be here where I am, hiding behind a plinth. There isn't even a door into this small equipment space, just an opening which makes it at least ten times easier for the intruder to find and get to me.

I guess the P.E. is cancelled.

Chapter 2: Intruders

I take a deep breath and tries to hold it as long as I can when I hear footsteps going into the gym. Male voices are shouting at each other and I hear screams as the intruders are pounding on the doors that lead into the changing rooms. I think it's just a matter of time until they get in, one way or another.

"Did someone get out?", I hear a manly voice say and another guy responds.

"No, we guard all the exits. Everyone's in the changing rooms."

I breathe out until the first person speaks again and I feel my entire body freeze.

"Not everyone." At the same time as I hear footstep walk off, I also hear footsteps approaching me, coming too close for my liking. I hold my breath and feel my heart pounding heart in my chest.

Please don't see me, please don't see me. Please-

"Well, well, well... what do we have here?", someone says in a mocking tone. I gulp and tilt my head up only to meet a pair of green eyes I've never seen before. He takes a step closer to me and I crawl back, but the wall prevent me from moving any further and I see the guy smirk in amusement.

"Problem, buttercup?"

I don't answer, and I don't look him either. Who even says buttercup? It sounds bloody awful.

When he realize I'm not going to answer, he gives out a low chuckle and stretches his arm out towards me to pull me up. I curl into a ball and let out a sigh of relief when I notice I'm just out of reach for him. The plinth is in the way, and I don't think I've ever been so glad about a gymnastic appliance before. He can't take any more steps towards me but the plinth only reaches to his hip and I know I am trapped. But I take all extra seconds of freedom I can get. I don't know what

he and the others will do when they have me, but I don't want to find
out either.

"Get up", the guy growls and I shake my head.

"No."

He sighs and looks annoyed, repeating his words through clenched
teeth. "Get. Up."

I shake my head and I can see him clench his fist.

"Get up now, or I'll make you", he threatened and I consider his
words but stay on my spot, not moving an inch.

He gives out a loud sigh and pushes the plinth away, and it lands on
the hard ground with a cracking sound, but I don't think it broke. I
try to get away from him when he reaches out his hand again, but this
time, there's nothing to stop him and he takes a hold onto my arm
and I yelp in pain. He drags me out of the small room and I notice
the gym is still empty. At least my classmates are still safe, for now.

"Hmm... and what am I supposed to do with you then, buttercup?",
the guy holding my arm in a tight grip says to no one particular. I start
to kick and hit with my arms and legs in an attempt to get away from

him and I hear him chuckle behind me. I stop moving and pretend to relax in his grip, and when I feel his grip soften a little bit, I elbow him in his stomach. He lets out a groan and I snatch my arm free and starts to run towards one of the exits. A quick look behind me states that he started to run after me, but at least I am a good P.E. student, and running happens to be one of my strongest sides. I reach the door and I am just about to open it when I realize it's the stupidest thing I can do. The corridor is full of intruders and I will just walk away from one of them and approach a dozen other instead. In the last moment, I turn around and head for the bleachers instead. The green eyed guy is now close behind me, I'm sure of it, and I have no time to waste. There's just one problem. I have nowhere to go. The bleachers are just a temporary place to hide, and with temporary I mean it will last for a few seconds. But as I said before, a few more seconds of freedom is better than none.

As I run upwards at the bleachers, I hear the guy's heavy footsteps closing in on me. I might be faster, but he is taller and have it to his advantage in this stairs.

I have to do something fast, otherwise, he will catch me, again. I can call the police, but something tells me that someone else already done it.

Suddenly another thought hit me. How is it in the other school building? With the cafeteria and classrooms? If the intruders can take down the whole gym, how many do they have to be to take down the whole school? I don't even want to know, and luckily for me, I am too busy to have anything else than to not get caught on my mind.

I take a look behind me and notice that the guy is close, really close. Before I think something through, I jump down from the bleachers and lands on my feet with a low thud. The jump wasn't that bad, but my feet hurt a little and I decide to make a run for the entrance door anyway. Maybe everyone is so caught up in getting the changing rooms open so that they won't notice me? Or at least notice me when it's too late?

I open the door that leads out from the gym, and I try to avoid the glass that's lying on the ground.

My heart skips a beat when I see the entrance door unguarded, but as I make my way towards it I hear a voice shout behind me.

"Stop her! She's trying to get away!" I don't have to look back to know it's the guy who hunts me, but just as I am about to push the door open I feel arms wrap around my waist and pulling me back. The grip takes the breath out of me and I scratch the arms of my capturer, who hiss in pain but doesn't loosen the grip. I am dragged back into the gym and I see the green-eyed guy walking into the small room I first hid in, and seconds later he comes out with a red rope in his hand and a smirk on his face. I understand what he's about to do, at least I think I know, and I start to squirm in the tight grip someone else holds me in.

"Don't even bother, buttercup", the green-eyed guy mutters and nods with his head at the wall bars a few meters away from us. I feel myself reluctantly being forced to them and the guy behind me forces me down on my knees and pushes me to the wall bars.

"Now be a good girl and stay where you are", he hisses in my ear and, of course, I try to run away. But he pulls out a silver gun and I feel myself sinking down to the floor again.

"Don't make me use it", the guy says in an intimidating voice. He has brown hair and eyes, and I stare him down as the other guy ties my hands to one of the wall bars. I don't fight back, scared of the gun.

I've never liked guns, I don't think they are fair. If you want to take someone out, you should do it in a one on one battle, not with a gun. The thought that all you have to do is pull the trigger makes me feel sick. It's not fair. Not right.

I stare down at my tied hands and stretch the rope, but the guy have done a good job and I can't get my hands out. I am in a position where I can do no more than wait and see what happens next.

The guys left me and I stared out of the trashed glassdoor. I can see the back of some of the intruders, and it seems like they have gotten an idea of how they can open the doors because they are whispering in low voices and nodding.

Shortly after, I hear the sound of a gunshot and screams fills the air.

"If you guys don't come out now, we will have to break down the door and that won't be done nicely and you will all get punished", a dark voice calls out and my body freezes.

"You got ten seconds to decide", he says, "and if you haven't unlocked the door by then, we will break down the door and shoot one of you, and we don't want that, right?"

I can see some of the intruders exchange amused faces and all I want to do is punch them in the face, but unfortunately I can't do that with my hands tied.

"Ten", the same persons starts to call, "nine, eight, seven, six, five, four... three, two..."

A clicking sound reveals that someone on the inside of the changing room opened it, and once again I held my breath as the intruders hold their guns pointed at the scared girls inside.

"All of you, get out with your hands on your heads and line up in the gym", some guy shout but no one moved a muscle.

"Now!", he says angrily and suddenly everyone starts moving towards the door and then continue into the gym. I meet Lindsey's scared eyes and her mouth opens to a big O when she sees me, but then one of the intruders tells them to line up against the back wall and all of the girls obey. I hear someone else from the corridor shout that if the rest of us student don't come out, they will start shooting down the ones they now got, one after one. All of the other doors opens and more students appear in the gym and lines up. Behind them, the intruders steps in and I count to seven, but I know there is more of them in the corridor, guarding.

"Listen up, everyone!", one of the intruders says and takes a few steps forward. "My friends here need some help, and it seems like you guys, or actually you girls, can help them. There're six of my friends here who need to find a girl each, and it's there you, my young ladies, comes in. We want the best girls we can get, no lazy ones with lack of competence, and now I am going to let my guys look at you girls, and see if they find someone they like. If they do", he says with a smirk, "you are coming with us. If they don't, we will just leave you with the rest. You see, we don't accept anything else than the best and I doubt we can find six perfect girls in here, but I would love to be proven wrong." He gives out a loud chuckle and gestures for the guys to move forward, and they all do and I follow them with my gaze as they walk to the lined up girls with smirks playing on their faces. I watch in horror as they rip the girls from the walls and gazing them from head to toe. Some of them scream and whimper in pain or fear, but the boys tell them to shut up, and no one of the girls dares to disobey them. I understand them. I am still tied to the wall bars and just when I start to think they forgotten about me, the guy with the green eyes crouch down in front of me.

"Hello, buttercup", he says in a cheery voice and I look away from him. From the corner of my eye, I see him tense up and clench his teeth in frustration.

"Don't look away", he hisses and I decide to look at him, only to give him a face that says 'I hate you'.

"Maybe I choose you", I hear him mumble and I shudder. I thought he would hate me after that I elbowed him in the stomach. Maybe he does, maybe he just wants to get back at me. I turn my head up and face him.

"Or maybe you just leave me alone", I say in a low tone. Before he has time to reply, a low laugh coming from someone else who disturbs our conversation, much to my delight.

"Really, Kirk? I didn't think she was your type", the new voice says and the green-eyed guy, Kirk, shakes his head.

"She's not, Vince. But I can still scare her a little bit." With that said, Kirk stands up and walk away. Vince gives me a crooked smile and bends down to untie my hands.

"It's not like you can escape anyway", he says and I frown.

"What's that supposed to mean?", I snap before thinking my words through. Vince laughs at my reaction. "You're just a silly girl. It's not like you can do anything to us." His voice is mocking and I feel my head turning a shade of red. Without hesitation, I raise my hand and slap Vince right over his cheek as soon as my hands are free. He stumbles back in surprise and when he looks at me I can tell he's not happy.

He lifts his clenched fist to punch me, but when he is right about to do it, someone takes a hold of his arm.

"What?!" Vince hisses angrily at the new person, this one obviously a guy as well.

The new face looks at me from head to toe. "Don't punch the face."

I look at him with my eyes wide and follow him with my gaze as his tall figure takes a step forward.

"I want her", he says in a deep voice, causing me to shiver. His hair and eyes are the same color as the sky at night and his lips are curled up in a mischievous smirk. He reaches out his hand and gently touches my cheek and I take a step back, my eyes full of anger and fear.

"Ah, feisty one, aren't you?" I hear him say as he leans in closer,

trapping me between the cold wall and his tense body.

Chapter 3: Kidnapped

"G-get away from me", I stutter and tries to duck under his arm, but the dark-eyed guy just smirks and stops me, putting one of his hands on my shoulder and forces me back.

"But, gorgeous", he says as he leans in even closer, his mouth brushing against my ear, "that would ruin all the fun, wouldn't it?" He gives out a low chuckle and a whimpering sound escape my mouth, and I immediately shut it. I don't want him to notice exactly how scared I am, but I think it's far too late for me to hide it.

"Aw, you're afraid?", he says in a mocking tone, "good."

I take a deep breath and meets his dark gaze. "I'm not afraid."

He moves his mouth from my ears and almost rests his forehead against mine. "Oh really? Then why are you shaking?"

I utter the first lie that pops up in my head. "Because it's cold..."

He raises a dark eyebrow. "You're a terrible liar, gorgeous."

"And you're a terrible person, idiot."

He tilts his head a bit.

"I'm not an idiot, I'm Nick", he says with an annoying smirk plastered on his face.

"Oh really?", I ask with played amazement, "are you sure you're not sick ? Because you act like a dick." This time, I am the one who smirks but my smile drops as fast as it came when I see Nick's face change from amused to angry.

Uh oh.

"Don't talk to me like that", he snaps and I press my lips into a thin line. I am about to talk back to him when a scream fills the room, and I turn my head at the source.

Lindsey.

Before thinking the consequences through, I kneel Nick in the stomach and run towards Lindsey, who is fighting and trying to break free from a blonde guys grip around her waist. Nick gives away a moaning sound, but I know that I didn't hit him right in the spot, he had realized what I was about to do and turned in the last second, but all I wanted was to reach to Lindsey and I succeeded.

The blonde guy holds Lindsey's red hair in a tight grip and she yelps in pain. I approach him from behind, but since I'm not the best fighter, all I can do is to kick and punch on his back. Someway, I manage to kick him behind his knees and he loses his balance and falls to the ground. Before I have time to do anything else, a clicking sound makes me freeze in fear. I turn my head and meet the barrel of a gun.

"Back off", an angry voice commands, and I obey without hesitation and slowly take a few steps back. Lindsey has managed to get out of the grip and I see her standing by the wall again, crying against Patricia's shoulder. Peter is a few meters away from them, and he doesn't look happy but, unlike me, he knows that there is nothing he can do so he doesn't try either.

Nick approaches me and gives me a death glare, and then takes a firm grip on my upper arm.

"You gonna get yourself killed if you don't stop", he mutters in my ear and I keep my mouth shut as one of the intruders take a step forward to speak. I recognize him as the one I think you can call the leader, it's the same person as the one who started speaking first once everyone lined up against the wall, the guy who told us all these other intruders needed 'girls'.

"Okay, everyone, sadly, we gotta move on before the police come and ruin everything. It looks like we will", he takes a quick look back and his gaze lands first on me and then on another girl from my PE named Amy, "take two of you guys with us", he finish.

I feel myself being dragged towards the door, and that's when reality hits me. They are going to take me. No... no, no, no! I start to panic and tries to get my arm loose from his grip, but he only tighten it and I yelp in pain. With my free arm, I dig in my long nails in his upper arm. Nick hiss in pain and suddenly stops, and I immediately starts kicking with my feet but he turns me around so that my back is facing him. He pins my arms roughly behind my back and as soon as I try to move, pain shoot through my body, starting in my arms.

Nick starts moving towards the door again and this time, I keep up with him, because if I stop, I know he will put more pressure on the grip behind my back. He holds me in the same grip that cops uses when they arrest criminals, and I know I can't get out of it.

With tears in my eyes, I am dragged outside of the gym building and thrown inside a black van. "You won't need this anymore", Nick snaps and takes my phone from my pocket, then he leaves me and the door closes behind me. I hear someone step in the car and start the engine. The car starts moving and I throw myself at the door, but nothing happens. I keep doing it over and over again until my shoulder can't take anymore, and then I curl into a ball and a few tears roll down my cheeks. I wipe them away with the back of my hand. Crying won't get me out of here. Nothing will.

Chapter 4: Welcome

I don't know how long time I sit in the van, but after what feels like an eternity, the car slows down and someone opens the door I've been tossed in through. It's Nick, and he gestures for me to come out. I stumble towards him with shaky arms and legs, and as soon as I step out of the van I start to shiver because of the cold. It's now dark outside and the snowing has started again. Nick drags me towards what looks like a big, old mansion made out of grey stones, and I feel snowflakes landing in my hair. I don't even bother trying to get away, because behind me, another one of the intruders walks.

As we get inside, the other one leaves us and Nick loosen his grip around my arm a little bit and start walking towards a staircase which seems to be leading down to a basement. Now, a growing feeling of panic and unease causes me to stop in my move, but Nick doesn't seem to care and he just continue his walk, dragging me along.

When we walk down, I notice the basement doesn't look like I thought it would. I thought it would be cold with no windows and only a hard, grey wall, but instead the walls are painted in a light beige color and decorated with pictures and the floor is wooden and polished. The only thing I was right about, is the lack of windows. There are a few ones in the top of the walls and I get an uneasy feeling when I see grills in front of them. As If I even would be able to get up to them without getting attention drawn to me.

Nick drags me through a corridor into another, and I eye everything I can see, which isn't much. It's just doors after doors, like in a hotel. When we reach the end of the corridor, he stops in front of the last door and takes out a key and opens it. It's now I start to freak out. He is going to lock me in inside that room. I don't even want to see what it looks like. Maybe it is in that room there're plain gray walls without windows? I have to get out of here, but how?

I do something I think I have to regret later. I slap Nick on his cheek and get ready to kick him in the groin, but before I got to put my plan into action, I feel myself being thrown against the wall.

"Don't you dare", Nick hiss inches from my face. I ignore his warning and take step two on my plan, and Nick gives out a moan when my knee hits his groin.

I thought I succeeded because he bent over in pain, but as I start my run back the same way I came, It doesn't take many seconds before I hear his heavy steps behind me.

Just when I can see the staircase in front of me, arms wrap around my waist and pulls me back with so much strength I yelp in pain, and scream of fear.

"No! Get off me, somebody help!" I take a breath to scream again, but Nick put his hand over my mouth and drag me back to the room.

When we are inside, he roughly throws me at a bed and closes the door and locks it.

I realize the room is nothing like I had thought. Instead of cold cement walls, the walls are painted black and the room is full of furniture. The bed I sit on is a double, not a king sized bed, but it fits two persons and is much more luxury than the one I got in my room at home.

The most significant furniture is a drawer in dark mahogany, a shelf and a flatscreen tv on the opposite wall of the bed.

"What'cha think?", Nick says with a smirk and takes a few step towards me. Immediately, I back away from him, but as I sit on the bed, I can't really go anywhere.

"At least take off your shoes", he says as he takes off his own, "we don't want any dirt in here, right?" I don't answer him and I don't take off my shoes, as soon as I get a chance, I gonna get out of here.

"C'mon, gorgeous", Nick says in a begging tone and takes a few steps forward and slides down next to me. I jump up, terrified of being close to him, and he gives out a low chuckle.

"Don't touch me!", I yell and push myself against the door leading out. My hands search for the doorknob, but as I find it I can't open it.

"There's no point in trying, gorgeous, you won't get out." I don't even need to look at Nick to know he is watching me with amusement. To my disappointment, and fear, he stands up and before I find a way to get past him, he has his hands on each side of me. He leans his weight on his palms that rest at the wall, and it's just a few inches between us.

"Smile, gorgeous." He moves one of his hand towards my cheek.

"Don't touch me!", I hiss between clenched teeth and turn my head away.

He stops in his motion. "I won't, if you take off your shoes."

I keep my mouth shut in a thin line as I think about his words, but then I realize I'm not in a good situation to start a fight, and I take off my shoes and gives him a death glare.

"Wasn't that hard, was it?" I ignore his mocking tone and look him right in the eyes.

"Why am I here?" I have really no idea of why he took me, and I wonder what happened with Amy, the other girl they took. And what if there is more than just us two? I mean, we were in the gym and there was a whole school invaded. All these questions give me a headache and all I want is answers.

"You're here because I want you to be." I roll my eyes and gives out a sound of frustration.

"That's not even a real answer."

Nick lays casually on the bed with his hands behind his head on the pillow. "For me it is", he says in an arrogant tone.

"Then why do you want me to be here?" I am desperate for an answer, and I don't care if my stubbornness annoys him. Actually, I hope it does. Who does he think he is? No one, and I mean really no one at all, has the right to threaten and kidnap young girls. Or someone else either.

"You know what?", he says and all hints of amusement are gone from his face, "why don't you shut up or at least stop asking questions? I took you because I felt like it, okay? You don't have to answer that, I don't really care if you are okay with it or not."

My mouth drops and I stare at him in disbelief. "I can't believe it!", I yell. "You kidnap me, drags me away from my family and friends, from my entire life, and you act like it's not a big deal at all! And just for the record", I add, "It's not okay." He doesn't have to know the fact that I don't really have a family.

Nick sighs. "Don't be such a baby. You won't see your family and friends again, buhu. You better get used to it."

Even though I figured out I'd probably never see my friends and foster family again, unless I don't get out of here, his words made my heart sink.

"No", I whisper, "You better not get used to having me around, because I will get away, and I will get you and your friends arrested for what you've done!"

Instead of getting mad, as I thought he would be, Nick chuckles. He really is a dick.

"Sorry to break it to you, gorgeous, but you won't get out of here unless I let you, which I'm not planning on."

My back is still pressed against the door, and I look at him with pure disgust. "Don't call me that."

He meets my gaze with acted astonishment. "Call you what, gorgeous? Since you haven't told me your name, I gonna stick with it and I doubt it will change even though you tell me. But, please, do tell me. I bet such a pretty face as yours have a pretty name too."

I scoff at him and become quiet for a while. He wants to know my name, but should I tell him? People always tells their names to their captors, but I haven't figured out why. Isn't it just plain stupid? I mean, what if you manage to escape? Then they know your name and can find you so much easier. I take a deep breath and answer his question with a lie. "I'm Sara."

"Sara?" He frowns and it feels as he burns holes in my body with his gaze. "It doesn't suit you. you don't look like a Sara."

I shrug and tries to act normal. "Well, that's my name, so obviously, it does fit me."

Nick gives me one weird gaze and then shrugs it off. It isn't like he can know I'm lying, not about this.

"You gonna stand there all day?", he asks after a few minutes and I glare at him with my arms crossed in front of my chest.

"If that what it takes to stay away from you."

He chuckles and gets up, in a few steps his in front of me.

"You gonna have to try harden then that, gorgeous", he mumbles in my ear and wraps his arms around me in an embrace. Instantly, I put my hands on his chest and tries to push him away, and when it doesn't work, I give out a sound of frustration. I feel his chest vibrate as he laughs.

"Sucks being the weak one, huh?", he smirks as he drags me towards the bed.

"I'm not weak", I hiss. My heart is starting to beat faster and my tries of getting out from his grip become more panicked, wilder.

"Relax, gorgeous, I won't do anything." I ignore his words and start kicking with my legs as he leans down on the bed. He still holds me in the embrace, which results in me landing on top of him. I finally manage to slip out of his grip and stumbles back from the bed.

He laughs as he looks at me. "Yikes, girl! I might be bad but I'm not that bad."

I lay my eyes on a black sofa across the room, and I make my way towards it and bump down on the soft cushions.

"Maybe you are, maybe you're not", I say, "but I don't trust you." It might look like I am calm on the outside, but inside I am an emotional chaos. I don't know if I am supposed to cry, scream or be angry. But crying won't get me anywhere, neither will the two other options.

I watch Nick in silence as he heads for a remote and turns on the tv. Then I drift into my own thoughts, which only makes my bad mood worse.

"Sara, huh?", Nick says all of a sudden after tens of minutes of non-speaking. I turn my head and looks at him, then I follow his gaze which lands on the tv. A woman in blue is on the screen with a microphone in her hand, and then there's a picture of me and Amy. With our names under our faces.

There goes that lie.

I listen to what she says, but as the news end, my mood hasn't changed that much. I know for a fact now that people are looking for me, but the woman on the news said that they don't have any clue of who it was that took me, or why. All they can go on is the descriptions from the witnesses, but that doesn't help much. For now, it looks like I gonna be stuck here for a while, unless I get out, which I am planning on.

"What's up with the grumpy face?", Nick says and I realize he has been staring at me for a few seconds. I shake my head and push away all the thoughts in my head, and get all my focus back to reality.

"What's up with your face?", I snap, "Oh, wait. You're just a natural disaster." I know I shouldn't anger him, but I can't help it. Sarcasm is my best defense, even though I know a little bit about self-defense, it can't help me out if this.

"What's up with your attitude?", Nick asks and turns of the tv. Uh oh. I don't want him to focus all his attention on me, I don't want him to look at me at all. I don't wanna see him, I don't wanna touch him, I don't wanna feel his eyes on my body and I really don't wanna be here.

But, I do really want to slap the annoying smirk away from his face. I want him to feel bad, feel at least some guilt over kidnapping me.

But does he? No, not at all.

When he realizes I'm not going to answer, he gives out a sigh. "You should go to sleep."

"And you should go to hell", I reply. I've been kidnapped and locked inside a room with my capturer, and he thinks I am going to sleep? Yeah, right.

"Been there", he says with a smirk, "but I was too damn perfect so they send me back."

I roll my eyes at his comment and put my arms around myself. I still got my 'leave me alone' hoodie, but as the night creeps in the temperature drops.

"Come here", Nick says as he sees I'm cold. I shake my head in response.

"No."

He mutters something under his breath and drags his fingers through his hair.

"Come here", he repeats, and I shake my head once again.

"I'm not going to sleep in the same bed as you, actually, I'm not going to sleep at all. Just give me a blanket and I stay here." I cross my arms over my chest to show that I ain't gonna move.

He glares at me for a few seconds until he finally gives in. "Fine, but don't get used to it", he says at he throws a black blanket on the floor in front of me. I pick it up and get as comfortable on the couch as possible, and then the Nick disappears into a small door I haven't paid attention to until now, but I bet it's a bathroom. He leaves the door open and I hear water pouring and then the sound of someone brushing their teeth, and I know my suspicions about the room is right. A few minutes later, Nick steps out from the bathroom and gives me a crooked smile.

"Don't even think about escaping, I got the key somewhere safe, and there is no way you are getting it."

The room falls into darkness and I hear him creep into bed.

Chapter 5: Business

I'm lying in the darkness, and I have no idea of what time it is. I think it's morning soon, but I can't really tell because of the lack of light in the room. No windows, no lighted lamps. Nothing.

I sigh and turn my head to the other side of the couch. I haven't slept anything since Nick went to bed hours ago. I just can't seem to get my mind blank enough to fall asleep. It's always something that stops me as my eyelids turn heavy and my body craves for sleep.

A part of me wants to stay awake, just to show Nick that no one, and I mean no one, controls me. But at the same time, another part of me is begging for my mind to give up and just give in and let sleep take over, because I need my strength if I am going to escape. But since my mind refuses to let me get even a few minutes of silence inside my head, sleep isn't an option anyway. I can get up and try to find the key Nick was talking about, but I don't think I will find it and if he caught me, I'm sure he won't be happy.

It takes a few more minutes until I finally makes a decision, and I sit up on the couch and tip-toe over to the drawer. I open them one after one as quietly as possible, but I don't find anything of value. Only clothes, clothes and more clothes. I dig through them in hope of finding something hidden, but there's no luck and I sigh and close the last drawer again. My head bounce from side to side as I look through the room. My eyes lands on the shelf and I quickly hurry over to it and starts going through all the books and stuffs on it.

Once I am halfway through, a deep voice makes me freeze in my motion.

"What the hell?", Nick says angrily and I slowly turn my head to face him at the same time I start back as far away from him as possible.

"What do you think you're doing?", he says with untidy hair as he takes off the blanket and sits up straight.

"I-I'm...", I stutter and takes a deep breath, "I am looking for something to help me get out of here, what else? You think I want to read any of your stupid books?"

He sighs and rests his elbows on his knees as he looks at me with a serious face. "I think it's time you learn the rules."

I look at him with my mouth open. "Rules? Are you freaking serious?"

"No trying to escape", he begins to say slowly, "no backtalk and most importantly, no disobeying. You do as I tell you, got it?"

I feel as I almost want to laugh. Does he really expect me to listen to him? After being kidnapped, dragged away from my life? I don't even know why I am here.

"Got it?", he repeats when I don't answer him. I look down at my feet, my hair falling down in front of my face as a shield.

"Look at me when I talk to you, and answer me." By the tone of his voice, I understand he starts to get impatient and with a few steps, he stands in front of me and lifts up my chin. Forcing me to look him straight in the eyes by putting each of his hands on my cheeks in a firm grip.

My icy cold blue eyes stare into his dark, almost black, ones.

"It almost feels as you trying to kill me with that gaze", Nick says with a tone now mixed with seriousness and amusement.

"Why can't I just go home?", I ask, not pleading.

"Because I don't want you to, and it's my will you are going to follow." I scoff at his words and turn my head to the side, getting out of his grip. He let me go and then gazing my full body, from head to toe.

"You can go take a shower, you look exhausted."

I don't only look exhausted, I am. Normally, a shower would be nice but under the circumstances, I rather stay where I am. Who knows what may happen. Maybe I'm paranoid, but I don't want to take the change.

"Uhm, I don't have any clothes", I say instead, hoping he will let the thought of me taking a shower go away.

"You can borrow one of my shirts." I am just about to protest when he put a finger on my lips, telling me not to, and then turning away and pulling out a black AC/DC shirt from one of the drawers. He throws it at me, and then basically pushes me into the bathroom and closes the door behind me. I immediately lock it and then turn around and take a look at the white room. It's pretty small, with nothing more than the usual. A shower, toilet and a sink with a mirror over it and a small cabinet on the wall beside. I opened the cabinet and saw normal stuff as shaving gel, tissues, toothbrush and toothpaste. Under the sink, it's a drawer and when I open it I find all kind of stuff a girl needs, makeup included.

I am just about to take off my clothes and jump in the shower when a thought pops up in my head and makes me freeze.

"Uhm... Nick?", I call out as I am scanning the room's ceiling very closely.

"Yeah?", he answers in a wondering tone.

I take a shaky breath before opening my mouth again. "There is no cameras in here, right?"

Even with a door between us, I can hear him laugh and anger heats up my body.

"No", he says after a while, "no one is watching you shower, I promise."

After taking a few more looks around the room without finding anything, I take off my clothes and steps into the shower. The water washes over me and I turn up the heat, trying to calm my tense muscles. It doesn't work that much, and after a long time I give up and step out, instantly being hit by the air that's chilly compared to the hot air from the shower. I quickly dry my hair with a towel and slip on my clothes, or well, all my clothes except for my shirt I replace with Nick's t-shirt instead. I have an uneasy feeling in my stomach as I think about walking out to Nick again. I know I'm barely any safer in here, but the locked door between us makes me a little bit more comfortable.

I decide to put on some makeup, just to drag out on the time as much as possible. As my eyes are sooty black and painted with thick eyeliner, Nick knocks on the door and shout at me to get out. I swallow and takes deep breaths to calm myself down a little, pushing away the growing feeling of nervousness and fear. I quickly cover the bags under my eyes and slowly open the door.

"That took time", Nick says and gives me a glare from the bed. I shrug and stops once I get out from the bathroom, not knowing where to go.

Nick taps beside him on the bed. "Come here."

I shake my head. "No."

He doesn't seem happy about my answer and he clenches his teeth. "Don't test my temperament", he says and looks at me to the spot beside him.

Reluctantly, I slowly move towards him, not wanting to face his anger. Once I'm in reach, he takes a grip around my wrist and pulls me down. Before I manage to slip away, he puts his arm around my waist in a firm grip.

"Get off of me", I hiss but his amused look is back and he only laughs at me.

"Seriously", I say as I squirm in his arm, but his grip doesn't loosen. What have I done to deserve this?

"Relax, gorgeous", Nick says and I do the exact opposite. He sighs and caresses my arm, giving me goosebumps.

"Why won't you just leave me alone?", I snap, showing him a glint of my anger.

He snuggles his face into my neck and gently kisses my collarbone. "Why won't you just shut up?", he mumbles against my soft skin. A whimpering sound makes it out of my throat and Nick pulls back with a smile on his face. He makes me feel sick, and all I want is to get out of here, the question is just how. I doubt he will let me out of his sight except from when I am in this room, which makes it all so much harder. If I get out from this basement I might get a chance to escape, but something tells me he's not stupid.

"You hungry?", he says all of a sudden and I am just about to say no when a thought hit me. Maybe he will let me to the kitchen if I say yes?

I nod as an answer to his question and he smirks and leans in closer to peck my cheek, I turn away in the last second and he chuckles and stands up. I follow him towards the door but as he opens it, he turns to me and shakes his head.

"Sorry, gorgeous, but you have to stay here. Don't want you to try anything know, huh?"

I groan angrily in response and he closes the door before I have the time to grab the doorknob and with a clicking sound, I know the door is locked. I try to open it anyway, but as expected nothing happens.

I throw myself on the bed and stares up at the ceiling and I frown once I see a camera in one of the corners. That much for privacy.

The feeling of someone watching me raises goosebumps on my skin and all my thoughts about rummaging through Nick's stuff washes away. I don't wanna get caught.

Nick comes back a few minutes later with a tray balancing in one of his hands as he opens and closes the door behind him. The smirk appears on his face once again when he sees me laying in the bed.

"If I'd know you would wait on me in the bed, I would have hurried." He puts down the tray on the drawer and I sit up straight.

"I'm sure you knew what I was doing", I say, "and for the record - I don't like being watched." I point at the camera on the corner.

"Oh, that", Nicks says as he hands me a sandwich, "don't worry about it. It's not on. The only time I use it is when I'm going somewhere."

I'm not sure if I believe him, but I let it go and stares at the sandwich instead.

"How do I know it's not poisoned?"

Nick laugh and sits down beside me. I move away a bit but he puts his hand on my lap, telling me not to.

"You don't", he answers", but I can promise you, it isn't."

I decide to eat it. If he wants to drug me - fine. I'll take the risk. I'm not going to be one of these persons who refuses to eat. If I want to stay strong and be able to escape, I need food. Sometimes food is your best friend and beats everything except music, nothing is better than music.

We eat in silence, but I don't drink the orange juice Nick gave me. I know the easiest way to drug someone is to slip something in their drink. He promised he hadn't done anything to the sandwich, but he didn't say anything about the orange juice. Besides, water works out fine for me, and I'm pretty sure the water that comes from the tap isn't poisoned.

Nick pokes me in the stomach, and a scream escapes my mouth. Not a scream of fear, but because of the tickling feeling his touch made.

"You're ticklish!", he says and laughs, and then starts tickling me. I try to stand up, I don't want to laugh, I don't want him to see a smile on my face, but he stops me and I can't hold it anymore. I burst of laughing, silently cursing myself for giving in and cursing him for doing this to me.

Once he finally stops tickling me, I am lying on my back on the bed with him over me with an evil grin on his face. As soon as his fingers leave my stomach, my lips curl downwards and he shakes his head as he looks at me.

"That much for making you smile", he says and I try to push him away, but he stays in the same spot.

"Get off me", I hiss, "and never do that again. Ever."

He looks down at me, looking me up and down with that annoying smirk.

"Kiss me and I may think about it." He leans in closer and I'm sure my face shows pure disgust.

"Euw!" I put my hands on his chest and use all my force to push him away, and this time, I succeeded. I sigh in relief and Nick just shakes his head at me, causing his black hair to fall down in front of his eyes. I notice he has a sharp bone construction, perfect chiseled facial features.

"Like what you see?" He asks and raises his eyebrow at me. My cheeks turn a light shade of red as I blush. I didn't realize I was staring.

"No, I'm just trying to memorize your face so that I can tell the police every single detail of it and get you put in jail."

He chuckles. "Well, I was going to tell you to take a picture because it last longer, but then I realized you don't have a phone. Too bad... for you." His arm sneaks around my waist and he pulls me towards the door.

"Now, gorgeous", he says as he opens it, "we are going to the living room to be social, okay? And don't bother trying to do anything. We are still going to be in the basement, and all the doors and windows are locked."

I glare at him in respond and squirm in his grip, but he only tightens it and reluctantly I follow him through a corridor and stops in front of a door identical to all of the others.

Nick opens the door and I get a nagging feeling in my stomach as we step in. I freeze in his grip as I meet the gaze of four other boys, and a girl. Amy.

She sits on a sofa with her brown hair in a perfect braid and she looks up at me with big, scared brown eyes. I notice someone sitting really close beside her as he focuses on the video game he plays with another guy I recognize as Vince, the guy I punched.

Leaned against a wall, I see another familiar face, Kirk, and someone I haven't seen before.

"The guy next to Amy is Will. You don't want to upset him", Nick whispers in my ear.

I want to go to Amy, telling her everything will be fine or just sit beside her. She looks sadder than me, she looks terrified.

I try to take a step towards her, but Nick pulls me back and I shoot him an angry glare. He leans in closer to me, his mouth inches from my ear.

"Listen", he says in a low, intimidating voice, "just do as I say and don't make a scene. Then I have to deal with you later and trust my, that wouldn't be nice."

My heart starts beating faster and he smiles, knowing he made his point clear. He walks towards a sofa, and I take a quick look at the room as I feel my body being dragged down with him as he sits down.

I am in a game room, with a big flat-tv, loads of video games, a pool table and a stereo as the most significant furniture, plus two black sofas and three bean bags.

"What do you think?", Nick whispers in my ear, meaning what I think about the room. I answer honestly and calmly.

"I hate it." The reason to why is pretty obvious, I don't like anything in this mansion. There is no reason to. He kidnapped me and put me here. I'm not a dog who you buy from an owner and put in your home, teaching them tricks and making them love you.

"What an optimistic attitude", Nick says sarcastic and before I have the time to answer, another voice speaks up as another guy steps in the room with a girl on his side. I notice her from my school, I think she's in the year above me.

"As all of the girls is here now", the guy speaks up, "I guess we can start." The guy who speaks has blonde, styled hair and an intimidating voice. He looks all of us girls in the eyes, sending shivers down my spine as my eyes meet his.

"I bet you all wonder why you are here, and let me make it short. I'm Zeke, and I am the leader of this... well, we're not a gang, not really.

But we are some guys, pretty many actually, who works together. You know, getting money, having fun? We're in the black market business, but don't worry, we're not some perverts. At least not all of us, and right now we just want money. And it's there you beautiful girl comes in. We are just going to contact your families and ask for a small ransom in trade for getting you girls back. Of course, we are not some men of honors and can't promise we will return you back to your families, but we are still going to take their money." He makes a dramatical pause and it feels like my heart is going to jump out of my chest.

"If", he continues after taking his breath, "we don't get the money we want, I can promise you that you are going to pay back in one way or another."

With that sentence, I know I am screwed. Doomed.

There is no way my so-called family is going to have enough money for a ransom, and even if they have, why would they lay it all on me? I'm not even their daughter, I'm just a kid they currently helping. I bet they are going to rely on the police, and I get a feeling of that the police won't find me. At least not in time.

What have I done to deserve this?

Chapter 6: No Family Equals No Help

My throat feels dry and it feels like the temperature in the room has dropped. Ransom. My so-called family won't give these guys what they want. I know it. What does that mean for me? Will they kill me? Sell me? Keep me?

"Relax, gorgeous", Nick whispers in my ear, "it looks like you've seen a ghost."

I haven't, but maybe I will be one soon.

"We already know your names", Zeke speaks out, "but it would be very helpful if you could give us your addresses too so that we can send your families a letter each."

He makes me wanna throw up. All of the guys in here does. All the time I've been focused on getting out of here, but can I really leave these other two girls? Am I that selfish?

A small voice in my head tells me that I should stay until I can get all of us girls out of here, but the bigger part of me says that the easiest way to get these guys arrested, is by escaping. It's that voice I follow. If I manage to escape, I can memorize the house and the way to it, and then the cops can take all of the guys and save the girls.

I tell myself it's the right thing to do. I repeat it over and over in my head. Trying to convince myself.

Zeke takes the other two girls addresses, they just give it to him, too scared to disobey his will. I understand them, Zeke is intimidating with a muscular body and piercing blue eyes, only a shade darker than my own.

Now, he looks at me with raised eyebrows. "And yours?" he asks.

I get a lump in my throat, not knowing whether to tell the truth or not. If I just tell them my address, they will figure out even sooner that they won't get any money from me. But if I keep my mouth shut, they might hurt me and make me tell the truth. I give out a sigh and meets Zeke's gaze.

"There's no point. I live in a foster care. They don't have the money, and even if they would, why wasting it on me?" By now, I have everyone's attention.

Zeke looks at me with an intense gaze, like if he's trying to figure out whether I am telling the truth or not. At least, he breaks the silence that has fallen over the room.

"Well, let's hope you're wrong now then." He says the words like it's nothing special, but I get a feeling of that there's an untold threat. I don't want to know what happens when they realize I am right, but I do give them my address, reluctantly. Once I have, Nick stands up again, dragging me with him.

"Where are we going?", I ask him, gazing back at Amy and the other girl I don't know the name of.

"Back to our room", he says and I stop in my movement. I don't want to go back there, and the word ours sends chiller down my spine.

"It's not my room", I state with a frown. Nick shakes his head at me and sends me a blinding smile.

"It is, exactly as much as you are mine."

I cross my arms over my chest and looks him straight in the eyes. "But I'm not yours either. You can't just take someone and claim them as yours."

Once again, he gives me a smirk. "But gorgeous, that's exactly what I did, isn't it?"

Chapter 7: Trouble

After that Nick forcefully had brought me back to his room, I'd gone back to glaring at him and just sitting in the sofa doing nothing. That lasted for barely an hour, until he gave out a sigh and left the room. Since then, I've been wandering around in the room looking for something useful to help me get out of here, but I found exactly as much as what I started with, nothing.

Now, I hear the lock in the door turn and Nick steps into the room again.

"Care to talk now?", he asks and looks at me from head to toe. I shove of the feeling of unease and just stare him down.

He raises an eyebrow. "I guess I have to make you then."

With that said, he locks the door and takes few step towards the rooms middle, closing in on me. I know I have nowhere to go, beside me is his shelf, behind me the wall and in front of me, him. I can move to my left, towards the couch, but what would it be for use? A couple of extra seconds Nick-free time, yeah, but that would also probably amuse Nick, or otherwise annoy him. Since I don't want to give him the joy of overpowering me, or being mad at me and make me pay for it, I just stand still on my spot. Ignoring the urge to back away from him as he moves his body closer to mine, only inches from touching.

"Talk", he whispers in my ear and I shake my head in response. Then, I suddenly feel him nibbling my earlobe and I turn my face to make him stop. Unfortunately, I turned my face towards him and his reaction was faster than mine. When I turned my head, he quickly moved his lips from my ear to my face, managing to kiss me in the corner of my mouth. He groans a little when I move away as he tries to place his lips perfectly on top of mine.

"Stop", I say, trying to sound commanding even though it ended up sounding like a whimpering.

I could literally feel him smile against my chin.

"Look who's talking now", he says in a mocking tone and I almost roll my eyes, but I'm too shaken up to actually do it.

If I like someone, or just generally think they are okay, I am a really nice person, but if there is someone I don't like, like Nick, I can be really sarcastic and rude. Luckily for the persons around me, I mostly don't hold an edge to people. Or at least I didn't, until a day ago.

Nice Alex have turned into sarcastic, lippy Alex, but I can't really say it's my fault because it isn't. It's Nick's.

I feel Nick wrap his arms around my waist and I try to squirm out of his grip.

"You became quiet again", he smirks and I give him an evil glare.

"Just leave me alone you freaking as--" Nick cut me off.

"Ah, ah, ah. Don't say it. I don't want such filthy words coming out of your gorgeous mouth."

I bit my lip, contemplating whether or not I should say it. I decide to do it anyway.

"Asshole."

Nick mutters something under his breath, rolls his eyes and tilting his head up at the ceiling for a few seconds before gazing back at me. "Well... I did warn you, and you just broke two of my rules", he says. "You disobeyed my order and you b--" This time, I cut him off.

"Actually, I just broke one of the rules", I say with a hint of flippancy in my voice, "because technically I didn't backtalk, because you didn't particularly say something. I just gave you a comment anyway. And you don't have to be so upset about it, I was actually telling the truth."

"New rule", Nick hisses and gives me a death glare, "no cursing." With that said, his mood suddenly switches again as he cracks into a smirk again.

"Now, I have to punish you and I think I know exactly what you need." His intimidating smile sends chillers down my spine and my heart starts beating ten times faster as he turns around and walks into the bathroom. Before I have the time to think about anything to get out of whatever he has planned for me, he comes back with a roll of duct tape in his hand.

I furrow my eyebrows and tries to hide the fear that now makes my body shake. What is he going to do to me? Oh god, what if he is going to beat me? Or even worse, what if he...

"Come here", he says before I can finish the sentence in my head. I look at him, with now pleading eyes, but stay on my spot.

"Come. Here.", he repeats intermittently, and something in his voice makes my feet slowly move towards him.

Once I stand in front of him, he takes a bit of the duct tape and places it over my mouth. I try to turn my face away as he does it, but he takes a strong grip around my chin with one hand and puts the tape over my mouth with the other. I give him death glares and he only smiles in response and roughly grabs my arm.

He throws me on the bed and picks something up from under the mattress. It's a pair of handcuffs.

Before I manage to get off the bed, he takes a firm hold on my left wrist where he locks one end of the handcuff. He locks the other end to the bedpost, and as I try to reach the tape that's covering my mouth with my free hand, he takes a hold onto my slim fingers and shakes his head.

"Don't. I gonna go get something, and if I see you without that tape on your mouth as I come back, I'll hurt you, physically. Do you understand?" I nod my head and tries to prevent the tears that are building up in my eyes from falling down.

Nick disappears out of the door and doesn't even bother locking it, knowing I can't get there anyway because of the handcuffs.

He returns a few minutes later with another pair of handcuffs in his hand, this one coated in a black fabric around the rings. He closes and locks the door once he got inside, and then he heads towards the bed and lies down beside me.

"Now be a good girl and don't scream", he says as he puts one end of the coated handcuffs around me free wrist.

"Oh, wait. You can't even do that", he mocks and then, to my dismay, he puts the other end of the handcuffs around his own wrist.

No... I shake my head at him, my black hair dancing around my face as I do, but all I get from Nick is a smirk. God, I really want to wipe it away from his face and replace it with a big, black bruise.

He reaches out his other arm to get the remote to the tv. He turns it on and flips to a channel that currently shows an episode of 'American horror story'.

"Well", he says and turns to me, "this isn't too bad, right? And don't worry, I won't do anything... disgusting to you, I'm not that type of a guy. The handcuffs are just here to prove my point. That you can't escape, neither from this house nor from me. So, this isn't too bad, huh?"

I look him in the eye but I do not reply, unsure of what he wants me to say.

"Answer", he groans and I shake my head as a reply since I can't talk.

"Good", Nick smiles, "because it has just started."

Chapter 8: Talk

As I am stuck in the bed with Nick, I feel the lack of sleep turning my eyelids heavy, but I keep fighting it and somewhat succeed to not fall asleep. We've been in the room at least two hours, and 'American horror story' has started to bore me. Not that I liked it in the first place, and especially not when something terrifying happens on the screen and my whole body jumps out of surprise and fear, causing Nick to laugh at my silliness.

Fortunately, he hasn't done anything else than giving me sneers and dragging in my arm that's handcuffed to his, just to annoy me.

Just as that thought flies through my head, I feel my side being poked and I squirm, but the poking continues as Nick's fingers dance over my stomach - tickling me.

I scream in the tape that's in front of my mouth, and Nick chuckles but doesn't stop tickle me. I kick with my legs, trying to hit him, but he then straddles himself over me.

Tears start to fill my eyes, not of pain, but because of how hard I am trying not to laugh. For the record, I fail. Hard.

When Nick finally decides to pull away, I think I'm on the line of blacking out because of lack of oxygen. I suddenly realize that tickling someone basically is the same as torture if you're in the same position as me. The thing I want most of all is to get out of here and the thing I want the least is being tied up, unable to move, close to Nick and being tickled. I think I start to prefer being beaten in front of this, at least I wouldn't smile then.

I scream for Nick to get off of me because he is still sitting straddled over me, but all that comes out is a muffled sound and Nick tilts his head and looks at me.

"You said something?"

Again, a muffled sound is the only thing that comes out, but this time, it is probably for the best with thought about the long list of cursing words I'm lining up.

"Ah", Nick exclaims as if he suddenly understands, "you want me to kiss you!"

My eyes widen and I start to shake my head repeatedly as Nick leans in closer.

Since my mouth is taped, which I actually am glad for at this moment, he pecks my nose and starts kissing my jaw sculpture.

Surprisingly enough, he backs off as I make a whimpering sound and I would've breathed out through my mouth if I could.

"Now", he speaks, "this isn't really a punishment, nothing compared to what it will be later on if you disobey, and I really hope you get it now. You're here, you're mine and you're not going anywhere. This special punishment, if you even can call it that, is just a one time only. Now, I will remove the tape from your mouth if you promise to talk to me? Okay?" His dark eyes are looking at me with an almost pleading expression, and I nod my head in response.

He reaches out his hand, the one that's not handcuffed to mine, and takes a firm grip around one of the corners of the tape. The following move makes me scream out in pain. He quickly rips it off with no mercy, and I automatically reaches my hands towards my face only to find them being yanked back.

"Son of a--", I yell but he cuts me off with a warning tone.

"Language!"

With that word, I shut my mouth and leans my head against the pillow behind me.

"Will you please get off me?", I ask as I try my best to keep the hate, disgust and fear out of my voice.

Nick seems to consider it for a few seconds until he finally gives in and rolls of off me and instead lies beside me.

"Now, talk", he commands and I frown as I look up at the ceiling.

"About what?" From the corner of my eyes, I can see him tilting his head my way and I look away as I meet his gaze.

"About you", he says,"let's start easy, I just want to get to know you better. Like, what's your favorite activities? What music do you like? What food you--"

"I get it", I sigh before he gets the chance to finish.

"So?", he asks and I turn my head towards him, meeting his expectant eyes. I sigh and take a deep breath, now when I finally can, and then speak out with unease in my voice.

"Uhm... drawing?" I didn't intend to make it look like a question, but it came out that like one anyway.

"Nothing else?"

I shrug. "Listen to music and hanging out with my friends I guess, but it's not like I am able to do that anymore."

"You can still listen to music", Nick smiles and I stop myself from rolling my eyes.

"Yeah, but right now I would prefer the other one."

I feel Nick interlace his fingers with mine and I look at him with a frown.

"You can hang out with me, you know", he says with a smirk and I slip my fingers out of his and scoff.

"Not helping." Does he really think I want his company? I would rather hang out with my school principal and trust me, he is boring.

"Well, the offer stands, and you don't really have a choice anyway."

I roll my eyes and instantly feel a pain in my side.

"Ouch", I yelp. He poked me in the stomach, hard.

"No rolling with your eyes either! Or any other disrespectful expressions", Nick exclaim, "and", he adds, "no sarcasm!"

I stare him down, give him the best death glare I got. Telling me to not be sarcastic is like telling me not to breathe. Or at least it feels like it right now, since sarcasm is my best defense, but I actually start doubting that now since it feels like it to more harm than good.

"I hate you", I mutter and tries to cross my arms in front of my chest, but then realize the stupid handcuffs that stop me.

Nick laugh slightly and shakes his head, causing a few strands of dark hair falling into his eyesight.

"You don't hate me", he chuckles, "you haven't just not yet realized how perfectly amazing and hot I really am."

I curl my hands into fists to control my emotions. "You know good looks doesn't make up for stupidity, huh?"

Nick once again takes a hold of my fingers and squeeze them in between his own.

"Luckily for me I'm not stupid then", he smiles but then put on a slightly more serious face, "but back to the subject, you said you liked music, what kind?"

I shrug. "I just listen to what I think sounds good, the genres doesn't really matter."

"Soo...?", Nick says, dragging out on the words, "at least you can name some of the bands you like, it's not too much to ask for."

I bit my lip as I think about what I listened too, it really was a mix of different styles.

"Dead by April, Paramore and Imagine Dragons." The thought of listening to music right, with earplugs in my ear and Dead by April on high volume, sounds amazing. Just being able to shut out the world right now would be worth more than fifty dollars.

"What about bands like Sum 41 and Metallica?", Nick asks and sits up, looking my straight in the eyes.

"Well...", I start, "Sum 41's cool, but I don't really listen to Metallica." Nick gives me a broad smile, showing off his blending with teeth.

"At least you got some taste in music", he exclaims and pecks my nose before I have the time to react.

"Euw! Can you stop... touching and pecking my face?" I try to rub my nose with the back of my hand, wipe away any trace of Nick, but he holds my hand and he is too strong to fight against.

"I will kiss your beautiful face as much as I like", he smirks, and suddenly he towers himself over me and I press myself against the bed frame. He puts his hands in his pockets and pulls out something small and silver. It's a small key, I notice, and my breathing becomes more regular again as he unlocks the handcuffs that keep me locked to the bedpost. I hadn't even noticed my breathing speeding up.

Unfortunately, he keeps my other handcuffed to his.

"You're not going to unlock the other one, huh?", I ask as he starts getting out of bed, dragging me with him.

"Nope", he says in an arrogant tone, popping the p. I stop myself from rolling my eyes and Nick drags me towards the door.

"Where are we going?", I ask and try not to sound worried, but I am.

"Up", Nick says, not giving any more hints. I stop dead in my track and he gives me a glare and tugs my arm.

"C'mon", he commands.

I look him in the eyes. "Will the others be there?"

"Yes", Nick sigh, "they will be there. Now come on, coward."

I frown but let myself reluctantly being dragged out of the room. "I'm not a coward..."

Chapter 9: Counting

We walk upstairs and through something that looks like a living room and then ends up in a big kitchen. All the furniture goes in black and white. White benches with midnight-stone colored tops, a fridge and freezer, microwave, coffee machine. All the normal stuff, just a couple of hundreds of dollars more expensive, and with a big island in the middle. Surrounded by five guys who immediately stops talking as Nick and I enter the room.

I want to sink through the floor or cringe into a ball because of their eyeing look but, unfortunately, I can't and Nick puts a hand on my back, pushing me forwards.

My eyes attach my gaze at my feet, which are all of a sudden becoming extremely interesting.

"So, that's the little rebel, huh?", an unfamiliar voice says, breaking the silence. Nick clears his throat and a small smirk appears on his face.

"Yeah, even though it doesn't look like it right now. I actually think she's a little shy", he says and moves his hand from my back onto my waist.

I feel my cheeks heat up by his words and I squirm out of his grip, earning a few chuckles from the guys around the island.

I can feel their eyes boring into my neck but I have let my hair falling in front of my face as a shield, hiding my face from the others.

"Does she even talk?", another voice, this one slightly familiar, asks.

"Like I said", Nick chuckles, "I think she's shy."

My mind screams at him, internally, that he is wrong. I'm not shy, but I'm not stupid either and I want to annoy him as much as possible, or at least as much as I dare to.

If Nick, or anyone else of these guys, want me to talk, I rather shut up. If they want me to eat, I rather just pick in it, clearly showing my repulsion.

"You didn't hurt her much, did you?", a third voice asks, not sounding really caring.

Nick shakes his head. "No, I didn't."

"Good", the third person says again and I furrow my eyebrows.

Was there a real reason to why he didn't hurt me? And if there is, then why?

Suddenly someone pulls back my hair and places it behind my ear. Reluctantly, I look up and find Nick smiling at me, not smirking.

I give him a glare before I can stop myself, and his eyes turn a shade darker as he sees it.

He leans in closer to me, his lips brushing against my earlobe.

"Now, what did I say about that?", he whispers and a shiver runs down my spine, and my eyes flicker down to my feet.

"Hey, dude", the third voice says again and I look at the owner of the voice. It's the blonde one, Zeke. He notices my stare and gives me a smirk and gives me a wink. I feel my cheeks blush against my will and I turn my face away from him as he continues.

"Why is she handcuffed to you?"

Nick chuckles. "She's not very cooperative, and besides, she looks adorable when she's mad."

I instantly open my mouth to say something rude, but I bit my lip once I remember the stupid, idiotic rules.

Zeke laughs slightly and turn his gaze to me again.

"Are you hungry?", he asks and before I even have the chance to say something, Nick opens his mouth and answer in my place.

"Yes, she is." I take a deep breath to calm down my tense nerves and the strong urge to punch Nick, or give him a high-five. In the face. With a chair.

"No, she's not", I speak up, not even bother to hide the annoyance in my voice.

This time, it's Nick who gives me a glare.

"Yes, she is", he repeats and I shake my head.

"No, I'm not", I press out through clenched teeth. I think I'm pushing his buttons, but he pushed down my own a long time ago.

Before Nick has the time to open his mouth to speak, someone puts their hand on his shoulder, catching his attention.

"Don't", a brown-haired guy who I recognized as Vince said, "if you are going to hit her, please let me do it instead."

I feel my lips form into a silent 'o' and I take a few steps back, just to hit the island.

"Relax", Zeke says lightly, "no one's punching anyone. At least not yet."

I look at him, his blonde hair is still tucked in a beanie which is gray and really worn out. A frown forms between my eyebrows. I didn't know if his words soothed me, or just made me more anxious.

"You want food or not?", Zeke asks me again, this time with a slight annoyance in his voice. I contemplating whether or not I should eat. I do want to stay strong and fit, they already got the upper hand and I'm not going to give up without a fight, but at the same time, I don't want to be drugged either.

Can I trust them enough to eat a small meal? My whole brain screams no, but I feel my head nod slowly as an answer to his question.

"Good choice", Zeke smirks, a disturbing smile similar to Nick's, "you're going to need all the energy you can get."

Nick puts a hand behind my back again, roughly pushing my down a chair. He then releases me from the handcuffs, thankfully, and turns around. He opens a fridge and fumbles with something for a while until he comes back and places a plate with a hamburger and french fries in front of me, alongside with a glass of orange juice.

I pick up the fork he gives me and shoves some french fries into my mouth. They are cold, and once I take a bite of the hamburger, I notice it isn't any different. I get a sudden urge of walking into the microwave and put in the plate and warm the food, but something tells me I should be thankful for what I got, and I get a strong feeling of that I'm right now am eating leftovers. Ugh.

I turn my gaze back to the plate, and notice everyone around the island are staring at me. I give out a frustrated groan.

"Can you guys just stop doing that?!"

"Doing what, buttercup?", the green-eyed guy I remember as Kirk mocks. I put down my fork with a loud clash.

"Stop staring at me", I yell, then instantly put a hand over my mouth once I see their reactions. I swear, their faces went from broad smiles to a countenance similar to the ones you get when you bit a lemon, and all in the short time it took for me to yell out the words.

"I think it's time we start", Zeke says and stands up. I'm not catching up on what he means, and I think the confusion shows clearly in my widened eyes.

"We're going to count to sixty, and you're going to run the fastest you can. We'll give you a chance to escape, so don't screw it up."

My mouth is wide open and I stare at him, confused and with furrowed eyebrows.

"What's the catch?" Instead of answering me, Zeke starts counting.

"One... two..."

I want to throw something at the floor, like the glass of orange juice I haven't touched due same reasons as before, but all I do is yelling at them again.

"What? Clearly, you can't be seri-"

"Three", Zeke said before I accomplished the sentence. I see a glimpse of sinister in his eyes, and as I turn to face the rest of the guys, they're all counting simultaneously with Zeke.

Understanding the seriousness of the situation, I jump off the chair and turn on my heels and start running as I hear their counting as a low chanting in the background.

Chapter 10: Hide and Seek

I instantly run towards the front door, only to finding it locked. Surprise, surprise...

Not wanting to waste invaluable seconds, I run deeper into the house instead. I start running of a corridor, and open all the doors I see on the way. Some of them are locked, and I don't have the time to take in the appearance in the other rooms, all I am looking for is a door leading out, knowing that the windows are sealed.

As I feel my muscles tense and stretch out, my question replays in my head over and over again.

What's the catch?

I open another door, this one at the end of the corridor, and steps into a big room with bookcases and a few tables, chairs and armchairs. It looks like a library, but most important, it looks like a library with a double glass door leading out.

I instantly run past a few decorative vases with green plants and push down the door handle. To my surprise, the door opens with ease and I frown. I had prepared myself for smashing the door open, shatter the glass into thousands of pieces. Could it really be this easy? I ask myself as my feet keeps moving forward and leaving the door open in the hurry. My eyes quickly glance through the new surrounding.

A few meters in front of my is a big, squared pool with a trampoline and a few loungers, and on each side of this backyard, in the corner of the mansion, goes a gray fence that disappears into the woods about a hundred meters away.

It is in the middle of the day, and the sun shines straight in my eyes and I have to put my hands in front of me to be able to see the tops of the fence. It's lined with barbed wire. Great.

Instead of immediately running towards the thick woods, I run to the fences and stretch out my arms in front of my to shake the fence, see if it gives in a little bit. Before I manage to slip my fingers into the gaps between the fencing, I feel a pain shot out from my fingertips and launching through my whole body. I scream at the shock and then line up a few curses as my whole right arm tingles in an unpleasant feeling. The fence is electrified, and not only with a few volts.

There is no way I'm able to climb the fence, and something tells me the whole place I'm in right now is enclosed by the fence. Running off into the woods will probably be as useless as trying to break a window or climbing the fence. Pointless, with other words.

Suddenly realization hits me like a punch in the stomach.

There's no escape. This is just a test.

They tricked me. I can't get out of here, not now with them in the kitchen, counting, and the electrified fence out here.

I bet they do this to all of the girls, as a test, or a game. And I bet they think I will run off into the woods, which is exactly why I won't.

I don't know how far they've gotten with the counting, but I do know that they will be done at any time now if they aren't already.

As my whole brain scream no, I force my legs and feet to take me back inside, still leaving the door open. I tiptoe over to the door that leads from the library back out to the corridor, and as I can still hear them counting, simultaneously shouting "54", I make a quick decision and open the door as quietly as I can, not bothering to close it as I slip out. They will probably search the woods no matter if the door is open or not.

I continue tiptoeing past a few doors and slipping into the third as I hear them all shouting "58". I'm trying to be as quiet as possibly as I close the door again, silently thanking the guys for counting slow, as I watch what kind of room I've ended up in. Everything in here goes in black and white, as in the kitchen, and I immediately understand what kind of room I'm standing in as I notice a washing machine and dryer, and even a white rectangular box that looks like a drying cabinet. I'm in the laundry room.

On the left side, there're a few lockers and I open them, just to find drawers after drawers full of sheets, pillowcases and other textiles. Realizing there's no way I will fit and that I don't have time to be picky, I close the lockers again and step into the drying cabinet. I let out a sigh of relief as I notice it's not on, and just as I do, I hear the guys shoot "60!".

I thought hide and seek was a funny game when I was younger, but now it has turned into a nightmare.

I can hear footsteps coming closer to the door leading into the laundry, but as I'm holding my breath as the sound grows stronger, the footsteps start fading out a few seconds later.

They just walked past.

Knowing that my hideout won't be safe forever, I wait a few minutes, with my heart beating more rapidly for every minute that goes by until I decide to step out. Someone opened the door once, a few minute ago, but they didn't search through the room, just eyeing it quickly.

No voices are heard, no matter how much I strain my ears, no other sounds except for the low humming from the dryer are heard,

I don't want to open the door, but I know I can't stay here any longer. They are probably looking through the woods right now, but they won't stay there forever and I don't want to be here once they decide to go back looking inside the mansion.

I slowly open the door and peek out, terrified of might getting spotted. The corridor is empty, and I take a deep breath before stepping out, closing the door as quietly as possible behind me, and then tiptoe through the corridor, in the direction opposite to the library.

At the end, it's a large door vault leading into the living room, which is adjacent to the kitchen. I peek out and notice the back of someone who sits on one of the sofas. The black hair only looks slightly familiar but I can't put my finger on who it is, but it's pretty obvious it's one of the guys, which means he is my enemy.

In the corner of my eye, something that's rising from the ground catches my attention. It's a stair, leading upstairs and not down to the basement.

Unsure of whether I should chance or not, I back into the corridor again, hiding from the guy on the sofa.

However, my temporarily safe spot didn't last long. In less than a minute of thinking, the sound of more than one voice coming from the library makes it to my ears. Oh no.

Suddenly, my thoughts become crystal clear as I disappear from the corridor and hurry towards the stairs, still tiptoeing but in a faster pace. If the guys coming from the library sees me, they will shout and caught the attention of the guy on the sofa, and if the guy on the sofa spots me, I have to run for my life, and probably do a little more than that too.

When I place a foot on the staircase, I'm biting my lips and sending prayers to no one particular that it won't give out any creaking sound.

Luckily for me, it doesn't, and I quicken my pace a little as I continue walking up, feeling very thankful towards my socks that attenuates most of the sound from my steps.

Now I got past one problem, and it's only one left.

Where should I go?

Locking myself in a bathroom is just plain stupid, even though it is tempting, but getting out of here is even more tempting than being safe for a few minutes or hours.

People say love is the best and most important feeling that exist, but I don't agree, I think freedom comes first. Maybe I just haven't experienced true love, or maybe I'm just a realist, but it doesn't matter.

I have a goal, and I'm going to do everything in my power to reach it, even if-

"Hey!", someone cut me off in my thoughts. It feels as my heart goes up in my throat and I take a scared peek behind me, only to find nothing there. I'm on yet another corridor, trying to find a place to get away or hide, but all doors are locked.

"Will, check the house! We're not sure she's in the woods", the voice calls again. I think it belongs to Zeke, but I'm not sure and the voice comes from downstairs and I ain't going down to check it out. I'm rather safe, or at least safer, unknowing than knowing and in danger.

I suddenly reach an end of the corridor and instantly starts panicking a little since I can hear footsteps in the stairs, probably belonging to the 'Will' guy who I guess is the one who sat on the sofa, but then a glimpse of brown catches my attention and I turn towards it.

It's another staircase, or not really a staircase, it's more like a ladder, something in between. But what it is isn't what matters, what matters is that it's leading upstairs, probably to an attic judging by the simpler flight of stairs.

Without hesitation, I start climbing up as a quick look behind me confirms my suspicions about my current stalker.

A squared hatch blocks my way, preventing me from moving further, and I fumble with the handle for a few precious seconds before I manage to get the hatch open and slip through at the same time as I feel something brush against my ankle.

I look down and my big, blue eyes meet a pair of gray ones.

Before I have the time to control myself, I give out a high pitched shriek and closes the hatch. Seconds after, he starts banging on it from underneath me and I look around the attic, landing my eyes on a couple of boxes which I quickly use all my energy on for pushing them over to the place where the grey-eyed guy will show up from if I don't do something to stop him.

The boxes weigh a lot and, thankfully, makes it more difficult for the guy to get to me, which gives me more time to figure out what the freaking fish I'm supposed to do.

A small window, different compared to all the other ones I've seen because of the flaking paint, catches my attention and I hurry towards it, ignoring the pounding from the guy as much as possible.

The window is full of a thick layer of dust, making me wonder how long it been since someone been up here, and I wipe the dust away with my hand, grimaces when my hands get all sticky.

Surprisingly enough, the window isn't sealed like the other ones and I unlock it with ease, feeling my lips turn up in a small smile as the window turn wide open.

Like I said, it's small, but it's big enough for me to fit in, and as I'm halfway through, I hear the hatch open with a cracking sound.

I don't need to look back to know who it is, and my heart begins to pound faster in my chest as I meander through the window onto the roof.

Just as I'm about to drag out my feet too, I feel a tight grip on my ankle, starting to pulling me back. I scream of surprise and despair, trying to yank it back without success.

"Let me go!", I cry at the guy, who just ignores me.

My hands search for something to grab and hold on to, but the roof is cold and wet, causing my fingers to slipper on whatever I find to hold on to.

Nick's shirt that I'm currently wearing is now wet because of the layer of snow I pushed myself through on my attempt to get out of the window, and now as I'm practically rolling around, trying to free my ankle, I feel the coldness digging into my skin and bones.

Maybe the roof wasn't such a great idea, after all, I mean, what if I would slip on the treacherous snow and fall down three stories?

The guy, Will, suddenly drags back my ankle with such force I slip back through the window and lands on the floor with a loud thud, and a heartbreaking scream.

He didn't just drag my ankle backward towards him, he also twisted it a little bit and even though I didn't hear anything break, I was too busy screaming out of pain, I think he just broke it.

He broke my ankle.

How am I supposed to escape from this place when I can't even walk or run?

Fly? I don't think so.

Crawl? Wish me good luck.

"Get up", he hisses at me through clenched teeth.

"I can't", I spit back, holding my sore ankle and trying to hold back the tears that're resting in the brim of my eyes. I'm sure I'm going to get some bruises from the rough landing, but my ankle hurt ten times worse.

"And why not?", Will snap back and gives me a glare, which I gladly return. Sure, I'm scared of him, but some of my fear has been replaced with anger.

"I can't", I say as I take a deep breath, trying to calm down my nerves, "because you broke my freaking ankle."

As a response, he gives out a frustrated sigh and rolls his eyes before crouching down beside me, slipping an arm around my waist and then standing up again, supporting me at the same time.

I feel uncomfortable of his touch and try to squirm out of his grip, but as I put down my sore ankle and makes an attempt of walking on it, I hiss in pain and would've fallen backward if it wasn't for Will's support.

He doesn't say a word as he drags me back the same way I came from, down the hatch, through the corridor, and down the other stairs until we reached the living room, where everyone else sits and waits for us.

"That took time", Zeke comments as Nick hurries to my side.

"What happened?", he asks and replaces Will as my support, leading me to one of the sofas and puts me down on his lap as Will explains the last few minutes. By a natural reflex, I try to stand up again once I'm placed on Nick's lap, moving away from him, but he just slips his strong arms around my waist, holding me back.

"Gorgeous, you're ankle is broken, you're clearly in pain, and you even bother trying to stand up in an attempt to get away from me? I thought you were smarter than that", he chuckles.

I give him a death glare, ignoring the so-called 'rules'.

"And I thought you were less of a jerk. I guess we were both wrong then." As the words leave my mouth, his grip around me tightens until it almost hurts.

He leans in closer to me, his lips barely inches from my ear.

"What's your tongue, gorgeous, or I have to hush it myself, maybe by using my lips?", he whispers in my ear and starts nibbling on my earlobe.

I close my eyes, just wanting to shut everything and everyone out, when suddenly the sound of a door being open and slammed closed sounds through the room.

"Dude", Will speaks up, "I thought you never would show up. You've just missed all the fun, but what do I know, maybe you already have had your fun with her? It's actually thanks to you she's here, we couldn't pull off the attack without you, man."

The newly arrived person gives out a dry laugh. "I told you she was worth it", he says in a familiar voice and my heart skips a beat of pure shock.

The blood in my veins suddenly freezes and my head start roaring like a waterfall. My heart starts pounding uncontrollably and all voices around me melt into a hum.

My mind tells me no, but I slowly open my eyes - and feel my heart sink like a stone.

Will said it's thanks to the person in front of the door that I'm here, the person said he knew I would be worth it.

The person is...

Peter.

Chapter 11: Sorry

"P-peter?", I manage to whisper once the shock settled down a little, but I still can't believe it.

One of my best friends, one of the persons who approached me on my first day in the new high school, who showed me around with a wide genuine smile on his face, have now betrayed me. Stabbed me in the back, hard.

I ain't gonna lie. It hurts, his betrayal aches in my heart, it feels as a cold hand has it grip around it, like it's going to crush it any second.

The moment I saw Peter, I could almost hear my heart break, not like when you're getting dumped by a partner, not like when you hear that you're friend have been spreading rumors about you, but as you figure out you've been living in a lie. All the moments I had with Peter, were they true or just an act? Does he care about me at all?

I know it sounds like my world scattered around me, like my heart been broken beyond repair, but it's not quite true, mostly it's because of the shock of seeing him of all people standing in the doorframe, speaking casually with my kidnappers.

I'm hurt, but I will heal.

I'm sad, but soon the anger will replace my despair.

I'm confused, and I'm going to crave for answers.

Peter stabbed me in the back, but I'm going to take the dagger and figuratively speaking shove it in his heart, and twist it. Letting him feel the same pain like me, letting him understand how much a betrayal hurts.

I'm going to get under his skin and crave for revenge.

I'm not going down without a fight, and I sure as hell can put up a good one.

Deep in my thoughts, I don't realize that everyone in the room is dead silent, not until now.

A thousand different questions fill my head, and somehow. my brain decides to ask Peter for the least important one.

"Does Patricia know?" If his girlfriend, my friend, is also a part of this, I don't know how I will react but I can tell you one thing for sure.

I'm going to have serious trust issues from now on.

Peter meets my penetrating stare and shakes his head. "No, she doesn't and I'm not planning on changing that either."

My heart feels a little bit lighter at his words, put he only answered one question and I got a lot of them left.

"And Parker?", I ask, not showing any feelings on my face. Honestly, I'm surprised I can even talk to him without breaking down or trying to choke him, but then there's my ankle, which hurts almost as much as my heart.

Once again, Peter shakes his head in response. "It's just me, Allie."

I flinch at the old nickname no one else than Peter and Lindsey calls me, but now when I hear it coming out from his mouth, it sends chiller down my spine and makes me want to puke.

"Don't call me that", I spit out with as much venom in my mouth as possible.

The anger that's boiling inside of me suppresses some of the pain in my ankle, but tears are resting in the brim of my eyes and Will, who is standing beside Peter by the door, notice.

"Dude", he says to Nick, "you should check her ankle, like right away."

I feel Nick move slightly as I haven't moved from my spot on his lap, and he places one of his hands on my shoulder and turns my face towards him. As he sees my tears, something that looks like sympathy flashes by in his dark eyes before it quickly disappears again.

"Let's go to the bathroom and get your ankle fixed", he sighs and I immediately start shaking my head repeatedly.

"No, I'm fine." I try to sound as steady as possible and not showing any pain, but Nick easily sees through my lie.

"You just found out your best friend betrayed you, your ankle is broken and you are obviously in pain, both mentally and physically. You are not fine. You're devastated", he states.

Realizing his words are true, I bow down my head and let my hair fall in front of my face, hiding it. If they are feeding on my despair, I'm not going to give it to them that easily.

I only turn my face up after a few second to send Peter a death glare, full of all the mixed feelings I'm having that are tearing me apart. Sorrow, confusion, anger, fear, disappointment, pain.

"He is not my best friend", I state in a whispering tone, "He is not my anything. The only thing he is even capable of being is a heartless monster, and he fills that role quite well."

Peter tilt his head a bit and keeps his eyes on me for a few seconds before speaking.

"Sorry, Allie."

That was the straw that broke the camel's back. With those words, he crossed the line.

A heating warmth quickly flows through my veins, anger, and this time, I can't keep it inside. I don't have the strength nor the will. Before I am able to control myself, I am shouting out my anger towards him.

"Sorry?! You say you are sorry? You're not sorry at all. But I am! I'm sorry I ever got to know you, I'm sorry we ever met. I'm sorry you're such a callously bastard and I'm sorry the air is letting you breathe. I'm sorry for Patricia who doesn't know what kind of person you are and I'm sorry I ever got here, and I'm sorry for your whole existence!"

Everyone in the room looks at me with open mouths, surprised over my outburst.

"Alex, listen to me", Peter is almost pleading, but his eyes are empty of feelings, "I mean it, I'm sorry."

I clench my jaw and shakes my head at him.

"Sorry for being the reason I'm here or sorry for getting caught?"

Peter didn't have time to answer before Nick interrupts our argument.

"Enough!", he said in a raised tone, causing my to jump a little since he practically yelled in my ear.

"We're off to the bathroom", he mutters and before I have time to say anything else, he puts a hand under my knees and the other on my back, and stands up, with me in his arms.

I start to squirm and kick with my arms and the foot which aren't sore, but Nick ignores me and just stride out of the room like nothings weird is going on.

Once we reach the bathroom, he puts me on top of the sink and I pout at him.

"I can actually-", I start but he interrupts me.

"What?", he raises an eyebrow in a questionable look, "walk yourself? I don't think so."

I cross my arms in front of my chest, anger boiling inside of me.

"I wouldn't be hurt if it wasn't for you guys!" I defend myself, earning a doubtful glare from Nick.

"So you are saying that it's our fault you decided to climb onto the roof?" He chuckles slightly and takes a soft grip around my ankle, his fingertips icing cold against my swollen skin. I flinch and yelp in pain and tries to take back my ankle by a reflex, but he holds it in a firm grip and won't let go.

"No", I hiss through clenched teeth as he stretches out his hand to the drawers under the sink and pulls out a white bandage, "I'm saying it's your fault I'm here, and if I wasn't, none of this would've happened."

I let him bandaging my ankle and I clench my fists in a weak attempt to hold back the pain. Everything is dead silent until his hands leave the bandage and he straightens up. I look down at my red foot, now wrapped in a bandage.

"Blame us as much as you like", Nick speaks up and eyes my as I get off the counter and tries to walk on my own, "it still won't change anything."

I curse as I put on some weight on my sore ankle, and immediately release it from the ground. All the people who say all you have to do is believe, probably haven't tried to walk with a broken ankle. Trust me, I do want to be able to walk on my own, but even though I'm trying my best, my own free will isn't enough. Instead, I'm leaning against the wall, standing on one leg. Nick watches me with an amused grin on his face.

"Need help?"

I shake my head in response, and - of course - he ignores it and closes the distance between us.

"You know", he whispers in my ear as he presses his body against mine, with the wall behind me preventing me from moving further, "for being such a beauty, you're really stubborn."

"And do you know", I say in a low voice as I try to ignore the lack of room between us, "that for being such a jerk, you're sure as hell also can fill the role as a possessive maniac too."

His gaze locks with mine.

"Why so?", he purrs in my ear and starts nibbling my earlobe. I try to push him away but almost loses my balance and therefore stops.

"Because", I start with a lighter tone, "you're a jerk, you're possessive and all of you guys here are maniacs, it's easy math."

Nick puts his hand on my hip, and this time, I do use all my force to push him away, but he stays on the same spot. He stays exactly the same except for a growing smirk on his face and he turns his face towards me again and with one of my hands, I push his hand off of my hip, but instead he just grabs my hand instead and interlaces our fingers.

I give out a sigh of frustration, trying not to show him the fear that I can feel creeping back. All the anger that have been boiling inside of me have now cooled down, being replaced with the familiar feeling of fear.

"I'm neither a jerk, possessive nor a maniac", Nick states. "I'm just a guy who lives to the fullest and takes what I want."

"And there you go again!", I complain, "you can't just take me and claim me being yours! I'm not a pet and you can't keep me here forever."

His eyes turn a shade darker and with his free hand, he starts following the contours of my collarbone, pushing my body against the wall as I struggle under his gentle touch.

"Gorgeous, I can do whatever I want, when I want it. And guess what? I don't want to let you go, so I won't. Easy math, huh?"

Despite the situation, I give out a dry laugh.

"If that's what you think, you're wrong."

He moves his hand from my collarbone and starts following my jawline. When he speaks again, his voice is full of amusement, not even the slightest serious.

"You think you can escape me? You're going to stay here, gorgeous, even if I so have to break you."

The creeping fear inside of me takes a few steps back and let the anger come back.

"Oh, I don't think I can escape from you, I know I can." Somehow, I manage to sound very confident.

Nick shakes his head, his hair falling in front of his eyes as he does so.

"Before you even taken a step outside this mansion, outside the fences, you'll be broken."

I raise my perfectly shaped eyebrows. "That's what you think?"

"Gorgeous, that's what I know."

I shake my head, my black hair dancing around my face. "You're wrong."

"Wanna bet on it?", he teases. My icy blue eyes shoot up to face his almost dark ones.

"Game on."

Chapter 12: News

I'm lying on my stomach on Nick's bed, listening to a cd with some rock band I found in a stereo. After my betting with Nick, he locked me down in his room again, and I've been here for two and a half hour now, which I know thanks to the tv I have on in the background in a lame attempt of trying to make everything seem as normal as possible, but of course I know it isn't.

I'm kidnapped. One of my best friends is one of the kidnappers. My ankle is broken. I'm locked in a room and even if the door wouldn't be locked, I still wouldn't be able to walk. Right now, my life honestly sucks.

And what can I do about it?

Absolutely nothing.

I've already searched through the room, trying to find something useful, but as suspected I found nothing.

I know I can't run away because of the condition I'm in, but that doesn't mean I can't get out of here. If I can't get to the police, the police have to come to me. I won't give up that easily, I won't let them break me. I won't lose the bet.

Therefore, I need to find a phone or computer. I need something that can help me connect with the world outside this stupid walls and fence.

But I don't think they are that stupid to just leave something like that free to me to take. They are smart, but I have to be smarter.

How I will succeed however is still an unanswered question.

I roll over on my back and hiss in pain as the movement made my ankle hurt. I focus on taking deep breaths to calm down, both for the pain and the frustration I feel over being powerless and not able to escape - yet.

The stereo shift to another song and I immediately recognize it, it used to be one of my favourite songs, and I almost starts laughing at the lyrics.

How come all girls fall for the bad guys? Well, I got an easy answer for that. They don't.

Kidnappers are -obviously- bad, but I don't have the slightest feeling for any of them. I don't like them, I despise them.

I hate them.

Suddenly I'm not in the mood for music anymore, and I sit up to go, or more like crawl, to the stereo and turn it off, when the tv screen catches my attention.

A familiar face is on the screen with a woman in her twenties standing in front of the face of the picture with a microphone in her hand. Her lips are moving, but I can't hear what she is saying so I grab the remote and turn up the volume to max. Now, the voice of the newswoman who stands in front of a picture of me drowns the sound of the music.

"Therefore, her biological parents have now joined the searching for their orphaned daughter who got kidnapped yesterday when a group of young criminals stormed into Beckwith High School and kidnapped five girls, which only two have been freed and returned safely to their families." The woman made a pause and a picture of a woman with chocolate colored hair and gray eyes showed up by the side of a tall man with short hair in the color of honey, and icing blue eyes.

The woman's hair is the same as my original hair color, and the icing blue eyes belonging to the man is identical to my own.

Realization hits me like a lightning. It's my parents.

It takes time for the words to sink in, but the picture remains as the woman continue to speak, but I can no longer hear what she says. I'm too shocked.

My real parents, who abandoned me when I was a little baby, just born, are now looking for me. Their daughter.

Tears are now resting in the brim of my eyes and I almost scream out loud when the news reporter disappears from the screen, together with my parents.

I've never seen them before, ever. I don't even have a picture of them. For my whole life, they've been nonexistent for me. They never heard my first word, they never saw me taking my first step. All they did was giving birth to me and giving me a name, nothing more, nothing less.

Suddenly, the door burst open revealing Nick, and I slip out of the shock.

"Shoot", he mumbles as he sees my face and the tv, puzzling the easy pieces together.

He takes the remote from beside me on the bed and turn the tv off, and then goes to the stereo and does the same. Then, everything goes dead silent.

"You weren't supposed to see that...", Nick says after a while, but I just look down in my clenched fists. They probably had the tv on upstairs or wherever he was, otherwise I don't know how he would've noticed the news. But it doesn't matter. What matters is that I saw enough. Not only the police are looking for me, but my parents too.

The fact overwhelms me, I've given up on them years ago and now they suddenly show up.

"Alex?", Nick says trying to get my attention, but I ignore him. Stuck in my own deep thoughts.

"Alexandra?", he tries and tugs on my arm. I only move away a little, out of reach for him. Of course, he takes a step closer and follows me.

"Allie."

I shoot up my head and give him a cold glare.

"Do. Not. Call. Me. That."

Something flashes by in his eyes, but before I get sight of what, it disappears and he goes back to his old, stupid, possessive, idiotic, maniac self, a smirk appearing on his lips.

"Fine, gorgeous." With those words, I groan despite the surprise and shock that still hasn't settled down completely. But I start suspecting that Nick got this crazy superpower, or curse, that makes him able to get on my nerves as soon as he opens his mouth - if it is to smirk or talk doesn't matter. Both ways work.

"Leave me alone", I mutter under my breath and turn my back on him. Seconds after, the madras I'm sitting on sinks down under another weight and I feel arms wrap around my waist. I instantly try to get up, only to realize the second after that I can't stand on my sore ankle, but before I even manage to stand straight on the floor Nick pulls me back.

"Gorgeous, I'm the one who's giving orders - not you. And besides, you can't even walk so what's the point with trying?"

I give him a line of curses as an answer and try to loosen his grip around me by using my own hands, but he just takes a hold of them too and soon I can't move. I feel his chest vibrate as he chuckles.

"Get off me", I squeak, not meaning to sound like such a baby.

Nick answers with a smirk. "Make me."

I'm boiling on the inside, but knowing that I can't win this fight, I stop struggling and he actually releases his grip and turns his body and face towards mine, a frown clearly visible on his forehead.

"You stopped fighting", he says slowly and I raise my eyebrows in a look that says 'oh really?'

"Congratulations, captain obvious." He becomes quiet for a while and it looks like he is thinking, and then his eyes lit up by something I don't recognize and he has a broad, amused sneer on his face.

"Have you already found your place here, gorgeous? I got to say that I'm a little bit disappointed. I've looked forward to breaking you. Didn't think it was this easy."

I take a deep breath to calm down, resisting the urge to punch him.

"I'm not broken", I state, "and I won't be either. I will get out of here, didn't you see the news? There are people who are looking for me, I'm sure they are looking for the other girls too, and you know what? They will succeed and you will finally be behind bars."

Nick 'tsk' at me and shakes his head.

"Gorgeous, you're such an optimist and I'm not the slightest sorry for breaking this. You. Wont. Get. Home. The other girls? Maybe, if their families cough up the ransom money, but that would still probably be a no. Two girls are gone, returned to their families. We didn't have any use for them and we got the money, that's all we wanted. But you? You won't get home."

I'm sure my eyes are big as plates right now as I listen to him with a half open mouth.

"But what if you get the ransom money from my real parents then? It's all you want, right? Money. If they give it to you, you let me go like with the other girls?"

Nick slowly shakes his head and his fingers start caressing my arm, leaving goosebumps behind.

"Gorgeous, gorgeous, gorgeous. You don't get it, do you? For the other girls, we wanted only money, they were useless. All they did was sitting in a corner and crying, no one of us wanted any of them, but it's not the same for you. And for the ransom money, we already got them. Your biological parents turned out to be pretty rich and we pushed the ransom to almost the double. Too bad they won't get you back, huh?"

Now, I can't hold the anger inside of me and I raise my hand to punch him with a clenched fist but he catches my wrist in the air and this time he is the one who gives me an 'oh really?' look.

"Remember the rules", he says with an intimidating voice, "this is your last warning."

My hand falls down lump beside me and I bit my lip, something I'm used to doing when I'm troubled.

"Why are you doing this?", I ask with a somewhat steady voice, "you got the money, why don't let me go?"

Nick takes a hold on my fallen arm, holding my cold fingers in his warm.

"I've already told you that, gorgeous. I want you, and therefore I will

have you. I want you, and therefore you will stay."

Chapter 13: Prize

It's getting dark outside, which I know thanks to the small windows that're placed in the living room I'm in once again. It's the same room as the one I was in when they told us about the ransom and when I saw the other girls, who I haven't seen since.

Nick, Zeke and Vince are in the room, playing some random shooting game on the tv.

Earlier today, after the news where I saw my real parents, they have told me a little bit more of who they are and made it crystal clear that I won't get out of here as long as Nick wants me.

They took the ransom money my real parents coughed up, but they didn't leave me back in return. They lied, but what could you've expected, really?

Besides that, they told me the catch with the stupid hide and seek game. Of course, they had known I wouldn't be able to get out, it was just a test. A test to see what I can do, and sadly, they told me I did unexpectedly well - which is a really bad thing.

No one of the other girls, they told me the other ones done the stupid game too, had thought about going back inside, they had all run towards the forest and when they reached the fences again, they'd broke down in panic attacks and started crying.

Quoted by Vince; 'They were useless. No one wants a crying baby who can't handle a single adversity or take a few punches.'

Right now, I honestly wish I would've acted like a crying baby when I tried to escape, if that would mean they would give me back to Carol, Brian and Lottie.

I'm glad for the girls who are now back safe at home, but I don't know which one of the girls that are, and which ones who are still here.

I've asked them what happened if the girls were 'useless', as they liked to call it, and had families who didn't have the ransom money. The answer had been terrible.

If they don't want the girls and won't get any money from their families, they sell the girls on the black market.

When they said it, my mouth had dropped wide open but Nick had put a hand on my back and started rubbing circles on it with his hand, telling me I didn't have to worry about it, since I belong to him, as he never gets tired of saying. Even though it's wrong in all ways possible, and absolutely not true.

I thought about ways to get him to hate me so that he maybe would get tired of me and let me back to my family, but as much as I tried he only seemed amused and he keeps telling me how he is looking forward to breaking me.

Well, I keep answering him with how much I'm looking forward to winning the stupid bet and get out of here and putting him and the other behind bars.

"Gorgeous", Nick suddenly says and drags me back to reality, "you wanna play?"

I give him a look that says 'seriously?' and slowly shake my head.

"Aw, c'mon. Don't be like this." He put down his console and starts tugging on my arm, I snatch out of his grip and push myself as far away from him as possible, which isn't long since I'm sitting on the edge of the sofa.

"Be like what?", I spit and look away from him.

I hear him sigh and move closer to me.

"Like a whining, grumpy three years old", he whispers in my ear and I turn my head towards him and pout with my lips.

"I'm not."

He flashes me a smile, showing off his perfect teeth.

"Are too."

"Am not."

"Are too."

"Am not!" I cross my arms in front of my chest and stares at him angrily.

"You're such an idiot", I tell him.

Nick shakes his head and puts two fingers under my chin, forcing my head up.

"And you're cute when you're mad."

"And you two are just too much, are we gonna play or not?", Vince asks, clearly annoyed.

Nick locks his eyes with mine with a small smile tugging at the corner of his mouth.

"You know what, gorgeous? If you play and win against me, I promise I won't bother you in any way for whole 24 hours."

With that sentence, he truly caught my attention. No idiotic, disturbing Nick for a whole 24 hours? Sounds too good to be true. If not, he knows he will win.

I give him a suspicious look.

"What game is it?"

He gestures to the tv, where a shooting game, in my eyes identical to all other games existing, is paused. My eyes widen a bit and I shake my head.

"Nu-uh. No way. I don't do shooting games."

"Aw, is the little rebel scared?", he mocks and I resist the urge to punch him.

"No, I'm not. I'm just not stupid. There's no way I'm gonna win against you."

Nick starts playing with my hair, twirling it with his fingers.

"Then I just gonna take my prize for winning right away."

"And what is that?", I ask and raises an eyebrow.

He leans in closer, his hand laying soft on my cheek.

"A kiss", he whispers, his lips brushing against my ear. I feel him moving closer towards my lips, and once he is inches apart from them, I place my hands on his chest and use all the strength I have to push him away.

He groans loudly as I ruined the moment, and I hear Vince and Zeke chuckle slightly.

"Damn it", he mumbles under his breath, "but now you have to play, otherwise I gonna double the prize, and then I can guarantee you won't get away."

I stay on my ground and meet his eyes which turn darker as I utter the last word he wanted to hear.

"No."

"No?"

"No", I state simply.

He gives me a look I can't read.

"You shouldn't have said that, gorgeous."

Before I have time to react, he takes a grip around my waist and pulls me down so that I'm lying flat on my back on the couch. He then towers himself over me.

I try to push him away again, but I can't place my hands on his chest because his whole body is pressed against mine.

"Get off of me", I start pleading, but he just smirks at me and slowly shakes his head.

"Not until you either give me my kiss, and it better be a good one then, or play."

I roll my eyes inwardly, but on the outside, I let out a groan and mutters a 'fine'.

"Fine what?", Nick smirks in my ear. I swear, if he starts nibbling on my earlobe I will literally punch him in the face and-

Oh no. Oh no, he didn't.

He just started nibbling it....

Second thought, I don't think I'm going to punch him, at least not now.

"Fine I'll play", I say through clenched teeth, resisting the urge to puke.

"Good", he says and quickly pecks my cheek before getting off of me and handing me a console.

I rub my hand against the spot on my cheek he pecked and reluctantly takes the console.

"Finally", Vince mutters and as I give him a glance, I notice he's not happy. I guess you can say he got a short temper or something.

"You know how to play?", Nick asks and I shake my head.

"No, as I said, I don't do shooting games."

"Well, you got plenty of time to learn now", Vince interjects and I shoot him a glare. Of the three guys in the room, I think I like Zeke the most. At least he doesn't say anything, or mocks me, or irritates me.

"Okay", Nick says and pokes me in the side, catching my attention, "this is how you hold the console, you're moving with this one and..."

I actually try to pay attention as he goes through what I need to know about the game, and as he is done, we start playing.

"You get ten tries", he tells me, "if you succeed with killing me once, you win. Otherwise, you know what will happen. He gives me a wink and I roll my eyes, and then focus on the big screen. One kill in ten tries, I can do that, right?

Twenty minutes later we're done, and I figured one thing out.

One kill in ten tries? I couldn't do it.

I failed.

Lost.

Nick won.

As the big red font with the two words 'game over' shows up at my part of the screen for the tenth time, I feel my heart sink down my stomach like a stone.

No. I don't want to kiss him.

Ugh.

Euw.

I'll rather kiss a frog and see if it turns into a prince, or a knight in shining armor.

The screen turns black as Nick turns off the tv, and from the corner of my eye, I see Vince and Zeke standing up and exiting the room, leaving me left alone with Nick, who watches me with amusement.

"Care to give me my price now?", he smirks and I gulp.

"N-no."

Nick tilts his head as I spoke, watching me intensely.

"Did you just stutter?"

"No."

He 'tsk' at me and motion for me to come closer. When I don't, he moves towards me instead and I feel my whole body tense up.

"Don't worry, gorgeous", he whispers in a soft voice, "it's just a kiss, it's nothing to be afraid of."

Yes, it is when it comes from him.

He pulls back a strand of my hair behind my ear and once again rests his hand on my cheek. My hearts pace increases and it takes all my will to not move away, but I know it won't be of any use.

I close my eyes, and seconds later, I feel Nick's soft lips connecting with mine.

Chapter 19: A Kiss

He pulls back a strand of my hair behind my ear and once again rests his hand on my cheek. My hearts pace increases and it takes all my will to not move away, but I know it won't be of any use.

I close my eyes, and seconds later, I feel Nick's soft lips connecting with mine.

I feel Nick smirk through the kiss, and it lasts for about three seconds until I pull back as he tries to deepen it.

I didn't kiss back, my lips were frozen, completely still.

My mouth feels dirty as if I just ate a fistful of soil instead of kissing the disgusting, obnoxious, irritating, repulsive, possessive jerk in front of me.

"Wanna do it again?", he winks and my eyes widen.

"No. I rather go and make out with a homeless", I spit back, "can we go back to your room?"

His eyes lit up as I mention his room and he stands up.

"Wow, gorgeous, I didn't think you would be that eager to get in bed with me, but don't get me wrong, I would love to get back to our room now."

I roll my eyes at him and stands up too. His words made me feel a little bit uneasy, but he wasn't serious, right?

"That will only happen in your dreams", I sigh as he slips an arm around my waist, preventing me from fall down since my ankle haven't miraculously healed in a few hours. "And for the record, it's still only your room. My room is at home."

We start walking back towards his room, and I get a feeling that he is enjoying himself right now.

"Gorgeous, this is your home now. And for the record, I do dream about it." He winks at me and I resist the urge to puke.

Please tell me he was kidding.

"You're sick, Nick", I mutter as we enter his room.

He walks us to the bed, but once we're there I slip out of his grip and slowly and painfully makes my way towards the bathroom by gripping everything I passed that prevented me from fall down.

Surprisingly enough, Nick let me go without a word and as I got into the bathroom I quickly locked the door behind me and reached out towards the drawers and pulling out a toothbrush Nick given me earlier.

Even though Nick just kissed my lips and never -thankfully- invaded my whole mouth, I put some toothpaste on the toothbrush and started brushing my teeth intensively.

I do that over and over again until I feel somewhat less dirty, and then I take a mouthful of mouthwash three times.

Nick then knocks on the door and I take my time before unlocking it and peeking out.

"You know I'm not poisonous?", he informs with a raised eyebrow and I roll my eyes.

"Ah, ah, ah!", he warns me and as I give him a questioning look he continues, "rolling your eyes is against the rules, and I've already letting it slip past too many times."

I cross my arms in front my chest.

"What are you gonna do about it? Hit me? Then go ahead. I'm not scared of you."

Truth to be told, I just lied a little bit. I mean, who isn't afraid of a possessive guy who kidnaps you?

"Oh, I've been thinking about hitting you", Nick smirks, "but then I realized it wouldn't work on you. No, I figured out something much better, and absolutely more enjoyable. Every time you break a rule, every single time, I'm going to kiss the perfect lips of yours."

I think my heart skipped a beat at his words.

"No", I blurt out before I have time to think, "no! You can't be serious. A kiss? Why not just hit me or handcuff me to the bedpost or something?"

I know it sounds crazy, me pleading and practically begging him to hit me, but at this time I rather have him hurting my physically then mentally. At least that's what my mind decided right now, but if it would happen, I'm not sure I would stay on my ground. But Nick hitting me would only make my hate for him grow bigger and bigger, and him kissing me would just push my limits when it comes to how much I can vomit in a day.

"I am highly serious", Nick says and once again slips his arm around my waist and leads me to the sofa, "that way, by kissing you every time you break a rule, I'll enjoy it at the same time you, in some weird incomprehensible way, are suffering."

I sink down on the soft cushions and he places himself beside me and when he doesn't let go of me, I try to pry his hand off of me.

"You know", I tell him as I struggle against his strong grip that only tightened, "it's pretty, or extremely, easy to be disgusted by kissing a guy like you. I don't like you, I hate you, and therefore it's pretty obvious that I don't want to kiss you. What makes you think that you have the right to even do that? Violate my lips? I'm not some toy or dog you can play around with."

"Oh, gorgeous", he sighs and pulls me close to his body, "you broke one of the rules again, didn't you? And to answer your question, I get the right to kiss you, not because you're a toy or a dog, but because you're mine and only mine."

His words send chiller down my spine and gives me goosebumps. I open my mouth to tell him, once again, that he is wrong, but he gives me a warning glare and I press my lips together before any words slip out.

"You know", Nick says as he starts caressing my arm, "we're not as bad as you think we are. Sure, we did kidnap you but what else? We haven't hit you, we've given you food and a place to sleep, a bed, but still you keep showing us that burning hate of yours."

My whole head, my whole body along with everything it consists of, want to scream to him and tell him how wrong he is.

Yes, they did kidnap me, ripping me apart from my life.

Yes, they haven't hit me, but Nick said himself he considered it.

Yes, they gave me food, but that doesn't mean that they aren't bad or that it isn't poisoned.

Yes, they gave me a place to sleep, in a bed with one of my kidnappers who forcefully kisses and touches me, who says himself he is looking forward to breaking me.

Is it really that hard to understand my burning hatred towards them?

All these thoughts, and I can't say them aloud unless I want to be kissed by Nick, which is on the bottom of the list of things I want to do, and highest on the list of what I don't want to.

"Giving me the silent treatment?" C'mon, gorgeous." Nick leans in a bit and rests his chin on the top of my head and I feel my body stiffen.

"Say something", he sighs.

After a few more minutes of non-speaking, my voice cracks the death silence in the room.

"What is there to say? If I tell you what I feel, I'm apparently doing something wrong. You may not see it, but all the rules do is preventing me from being myself. I'm a backtalker, okay? I'm sarcastic at times when I'm uncomfortable or annoyed. I don't like being told what to do and I sure as hell don't want to kiss you."

I expect him to try to slap kiss me, but he doesn't and that makes me look at him with a questioning look written on my face.

"You don't have to be afraid of me", Nick says and stares at me intensively, his dark eyes boring into my icing blue.

"I'm not", I whisper, "I'm uncomfortable and annoyed."

He brushes away the hair that has fallen in front of my eyes and leaves his hand cupping my cheek.

"You're lying, but you don't have to be afraid. I won't hurt you as long as I don't have to, and that's all up to you."

I furrow my eyebrows together. Where did his cocky attitude go? Does he really think a short nice, or more like nicer, act will change anything? Because it won't.

"If you aren't going to say anything, we might as well go to bed", Nick says and sighs again.

I don't answer him as he stands up and head into the bathroom, after locking the door leading out to the corridor and flashing me a small smile.

It's not like I'm able to walk anywhere anyway.

I can hear the tap go on and off in the bathroom and I rest my head in my hands.

How did I get into this mess? What have I ever done to deserve this?

I've never been a goody two-shoes, but not the opposite either. I've done bad things, I've made mistakes but they haven't been life changing.

Sadly, meeting Peter might have been.

I still can't really believe it, after all, the time we spent together he just stabs me in the back.

At least I still have Lindsey. She wouldn't turn her back on me. That's something I'm sure of, hundred percent. I hope with all my heart that I'm right. Only the thought of Lindsey leaving me is unbearable.

An unnoticed tear slips down my cheek and I leave it, not bother to wipe it away.

I just sit on the sofa for a while, deep in my thoughts about Lindsey and my old life, which makes my heart ache because of how much I miss it even though it wasn't more than almost two days ago it got ripped apart from me, and Nick comes in at some point.

I don't notice him until my tired eyes flatten over the room and lands on him, who is leaning against the wall, watching me.

"Tired, huh?"

I realize I haven't slept in a very long time since I didn't get any sleep at all on the couch, maybe the fear and my tense body have kept me awake the whole day, along with the pain in my ankle which I think is the main reason.

Lucky for me, they gave me some advil when we were in the living room and the effect still haven't worn out.

I think my face is answer enough to his question, and without any more words said Nick helps me to the bathroom and gives me a big shirt to sleep in.

"Don't you have any sweatpants or shorts?", I ask and let a bit of my attitude come back.

Nick gives out a long sigh.

"Do you really need it? Isn't the shirt enough?"

I shake my head in response and he groans, mutters something that sounds like 'wait here', and exits the room.

In the meantime, I place myself in front of the mirror and brushes my hair before I start braiding it. By the time I'm done and have my hair in a decent fishtail braid, Nick comes back with a few clothes in his hand.

He puts some of them in the drawer and then gives me a purple pair of shorts, which I gladly take before closing the door in his face.

I slip on his shirt, this one with a big 'Iron Maiden' print on the chest. I then reach for the shorts and notice that there is a clean pair of panties too, and I quickly change and put my dirty clothes in a hamper placed in the corner of the bathroom.

The shorts is too short for my taste, it barely reaches down my mid thigh, but then what could you expect from someone like Nick?

I slowly peek out the door and notice that everything is laying in darkness. A sigh of relief escape my lips and I quickly turn off the lights in the bathroom and steps out, supporting myself against the wall as I do so.

Now I just have to make it to the couch someho-

Arms slips around my waist, interrupting my thought and causing me to jump.

"Not so fast, gorgeous", Nick whispers in my ear. Fast? Ha, what a joke.

"Tonight, you're sleeping with me", he states and I think he could feel my body stiffen because seconds later, he gives out a low chuckle causing his chest to vibrate.

"I won't do anything if that's what you're afraid of. But...", he makes a dramatic pause as he leads me to the bed, "I want to be able to see, hear and touch you."

"That doesn't sound creepy at all...", I mutter under my breath, hoping he wouldn't hear.

Of course, he did.

"Gorgeous, you practically begging for punishment."

I feel the soft material of the sheets as we sit down.

"No", I whisper, "please don't. I wasn't eve-"

Lips connecting with mine cuts me off. It's a miracle he even found them in the dark.

My back falls down on the mattress as Nick towers himself over me, but I jerk my head to the side and break off the kiss.

Even though I can't see, I'm sure Nick have a smirk plastered on his face right now as my own lips are curled downwards.

I try to get up, moving back to the bathroom to brush my teeth again, but Nick holds me down.

"Don't. You better get used to it anyway because with that attitude of your, this will happen on regular basis."

I'm fuming on the inside and have to prevent myself from letting out a long line of curse words, therefore I keep my mouth shut as we get under the covers and Nick slips an arm around my waist.

I try to take his arm off of me, but he only pulls me closer to his chest, which I now notice is bare.

"You wanna fight or sleep?", he mumbles in my ear and my whole brain screams fight, but my whole body screams sleep. My eyelids keep falling down and I let out a small yawn I couldn't prevent from escaping my lips.

Nick moves his arm from my waist to my arm and starts caressing it, his fingertips moving up and down my upper arm, causing goose-bumps to rise.

If there was someone else, anyone, who would do that, I may have found it soothing but Nick only makes me feel uncomfortable.

"Goodnight, gorgeous", he whispers and continues caressing my arm. It doesn't take long before my eyelids betray me and I drift off to sleep.

Chapter 15: Keeping The Enemy Close

It's been three days since I hurt my ankle, and nothing special has happened since. I've kept my mouth shut most of the time, giving Nick the silent treatment, and somehow managed to stay out of trouble.

Oh, and it was shown that my ankle wasn't broken, just sprained, and it's healing surprisingly fast. I can't really understand how it could hurt so much and still be almost completely healed by now. I can walk on it, but it does hurt a little bit, but I don't complain. Actually, I think it's time for me to try to get out of here. Not that I haven't thought or tried before, but with a sprained ankle you don't get far and I've kept my eyes open for a phone or computer, but without any luck.

But now my patient is running out and I don't know how much longer I can put up with Nick and his arrogant, cocky, obnoxious attitude.

I've said it before, and I'm going to say it again. If I won't get to the police, the police have to come here and this time, I won't just keep it in mind, I will make it true.

I'm tired of waiting, I'm tired of not being able to say what I want and being myself. I'm tired of being here, and I want to get home.

This time, I won't just put up a fight, I will win too.

And I'm going to start with plan A - getting under Peter's skin.

I haven't spoken to him since I found out what he did, and trust me, I don't want to break the silence which is laying comfortable between us. I don't want to break the ice, but I'm afraid I have to.

Maybe, just maybe, Peter isn't a complete douchebag. Maybe he does, or did, consider me as his friend and had some friendly feeling towards me. I really hope he did, because that's what my plan is built on.

I'm going to talk to him, telling him I want to forget what happened and start over, that I need a friend here, and hopefully he will fall for it.

I need to get him on my side, or at least somewhere between my side and the others, and I'm going to start the plan right... now.

It's afternoon, and I'm sitting in the living room all by myself. And no, it's not because they trust me, it's because there's absolutely no way leading out from this basement and the other guys are upstairs and probably watching my every move on a camera.

Nooo, not creepy at all *cough*.

I get up from the sofa and turn off the tv, there wasn't anything worth watching anyway, and make my way upstairs.

I find the guys in the main living room, which is the big one where Will sat when I tried to escape, and as I get everyone turns their attention towards me and I feel my cheeks blush slightly and I decide not to try to hide it and use it to my advantage instead.

Normally, I would hide all feelings from my face and walk with my head raised high, but now I do the opposite instead and as I make my way to the guys, I keep staring at me feet.

I stop in front of Peter, who is sitting with his phone in his hand.

"Uhm...", I mumble as I start tugging my lip, "c-can we talk?" I ask, stuttering on purpose. I hate playing weak, but if it can take me out of this hell hole, I'm gladly doing it.

Peter looks at me with a confused face and furrowed eyebrows.

"Ehm... yeah, sure." He stands up and seems to be extremely uncomfortable, which makes me smile a little on the inside.

"Let's go to my room...", he mumbles and starts walking upstairs. I follow him and feel the other guys' burning stares on my neck.

His room is close to the stairs and as we get in, I stand awkwardly by the door as he sits down on his bed. After a few seconds of awkward silence, he pats on the spot beside him and I slowly sit down beside him.

"So... what do you wanna talk about?" he says and breaks the silence.

I feel my eyes becoming glossy, a part of the act, and I meet his gaze with tears in my eyes and a quivering bottom lip.

"D-did you ever consider me your f-friend? O-or was it... was it all just an a-act?" The question is real, and I do want an answer.

Peter sighs.

"Allie", I'm trying not to flinch at the nickname, "you were always my friend. I didn't want them to take you in the first place but I can't tell them what to do and not to."

His words make me feel a little bit, but only a little bit, better.

"S-so you're s-still my... friend?", I stutter and wipe away a falling tear.

"If you want me to be", he says in a low voice, "but I don't understand your sudden change of mood. I really want to believe you, but you've been avoiding me for days and I know you, Allie. You never cry or gives in, let alone forgiving someone just like that."

Shoot. He can't see through my lie, he just can't.

Shoot. Shoot. Shoot.

"I-I've changed. This place is s-scary and I miss my h-home. You're all I got left from it, from home..."

I'm not sure he buys my act and I decide to take a big risk.

I bury my head in my hands and burst into tears, letting them fall freely down my cheeks.

As Peter put an arm around my shoulders, I smile into my hands and know I succeeded.

"Shh...", he whispers and starts rocking me back and forth. After a few minutes, I pull away sobbing and with reddened eyes.

"You want anything?", Peter asks worriedly, "tea? coffee? Anything?"

I give him an attempt of a small smile.

"Tea, p-please."

"Alright", he says and stands up, "wait here, I'll be back in a bit, okay?"

I nod my head in response and watch him leaving the room. As soon as his back disappears from my view, I wipe away a few remaining tears and starts scanning the room.

My eyes immediately land on a small, rectangular object on the bed.

His phone.

Bingo.

Chapter 16: Lies

I watch the phone with my mouth slightly opened.

Could it really be that easy?

It's just laying there, taunting me.

Daring me to pick it up.

I expected it to be much harder than this, but this was what I planned for.

Getting his phone.

It's daring me to pick it up, and I do.

As I turn on the screen, I hear someone clear his throat.

My whole body freezes and it feels as my heart skipped a beat.

Slowly, I turn around with the phone in my hand and meets the gaze of Peter.

"P-peter", I stutter, this time not on purpose, "I can expl-"

"Cut the crap, Allie", he spits out with venom in his voice. "Don't even try to wiggle yourself out of this. You really think I would be fooled by your act? C'mon, I know you better than that."

I stare at him in disbelief. The Peter I talked to a minute ago has washed away completely and been replaced by a cold shell of what he once was, or at least what he once pretended to be.

"You... you played me...", I whisper, still taken aback.

Peter gives out a dry laugh.

"Yeah, yeah, yeah. The player got played, you failed at your own game."

I bite my lip and take deep breaths, focusing on controlling the anger that's burning inside of me. The anger and hate I felt before which had cooled down, have now been lit again.

"You think this is a game?" I spit out, "you think I'm doing this for fun, huh? I'm doing this because I don't want to be here because I want to get back to what you've ripped me away from."

Peter's face and eyes are emotionless and plain blank, not showing anything at all.

"Too bad", he says slowly, "because you ain't going anywhere."

With those words, he declared war.

I wanted to rose up from my place on the bed and wipe the tugging smirk off his lips, make him feel the pain I do.

But I don't, because somewhere in the chaos of my anger, I still have some sense left.

With Peter's phone in my hand, I turn on the screen with calling the emergency in my mind, but before I have time to put my plan into action Peter throws himself over me, and I react too late.

I tried to slip out of the bed, but he got a hold of my upper arm and hold me back, but I didn't let go of the phone.

It's in my hand, still, and I try to put one of my shaking fingers on the call icon, but fails.

"Not so fast", Peter hisses and the pressure of the grip on my arm increases immediately.

I scream in pain and reluctantly let go of the phone, which lands on the floor with a thud.

With my free hand, I reach after it but Peter kicks it under the bed with one of his feet, and we start wrestling each other.

It didn't take long before I was lying on the bed on my back with Peter above me, pinning me down.

And just in that moment, the door burst open and both of our gazes snapped there.

"What the hell?", Nick shouts from the doorway, his eyes wide opened.

I can only imagine what this must look like in his eyes, me lying on Peter's bed with him practically all over me.

Even the thought of it made me shudder, but I suddenly realized I could use this to my advantage.

"Dude", Peter speaks up with an almost pleading face, "it's not what it looks like. I can explain, we ju-"

"He kissed me", I blurted out before Peter had time to finish, and they both turned their attention towards me, eyes widened and flushed cheeks. Nick's cheeks because of anger, Peter's because of embarrassment, and his eyes full of worry and confusion.

Of course, I just lied.

He didn't kiss me.

Ugh.

But Nick doesn't have to know that.

"Nick...", Peter says in a slow tone, "she's lying. Promise. Why would I even kiss her? I have a girlfriend for freaking sake!"

I decide to continue my act, and I furrow my eyebrows together.

"That haven't stopped you before. You've always had a tiny crush on my, don't you remember last spring break? You tried to kiss me."

I have to stop myself from smiling, proud of my little act. Of course, he doesn't have a crush on me and when it comes to what I just said about last spring break?

Just a lie.

Peter's head shot up once I uttered the lie, and he began shaking his head repeatedly.

"That's not true, Nick. C'mon you know me, I would nev-"

"Get off of her", Nick cuts off, and Peter immediately does as he says, still rambling excuses and defending himself, repeating that he would never cheat on Patricia.

Even though I despite Peter now, I do give him extra credit for staying true to his girlfriend, who is also my friend.

"She tried to escape!", he suddenly yells out, and Nick freezes in the steps he started taking towards me.

"He tried to kiss me!", I plead with tears in my eyes."

Nick gives out a frustrated sigh and gives us both suspicious glares.

"Which one of you is lying and who is telling the truth?"

I open my mouth at the same time as Peter, and we both start defending ourselves again.

After a while, he tells us both to shut up, being more serious than ever.

"I don't want to hear more of this. I just want to know who is lying, because I can tell you that whoever it is out of you two, the responsible won't like the consequences."

Shoot.

"So, care to tell me now?"

Chapter 17: Guilty

"I'm done listening to your bullshit", Nick tell both Peter and me and I can feel my cheeks wanting to turn crimson, but I have resisted it the past half an hour and I'm not planning on letting the bars fall down now.

Nick still doesn't know that I'm lying, and I'm trying my best to keep it that way, but Peter does everything in his power to get me caught.

I can't blame him, though.

What Nick has planned for the guilty one is still unknown, but what I do know is that neither Peter nor I want to find out, but the time is ticking and Nicks patient is running out.

We're sitting in the living room in the basement, and I sit on a couch with Peter by my side, and Nick and Zeke are staring at us from across the room, their gazes almost burning through my skin.

Zeke hasn't said anything to us at all, Nick has done all the talking, but now it seems as it isn't only Nick's patient that's running low, cause for the first time since Zeke stepped into this room twenty minutes ago, he speaks up.

"Here's the thing", he starts and make a pause to look both of us in the eye, "I've been sitting here for a while, and both of you keep going on and on about why you're innocent, but one of you is clearly lying, and if there're two things I don't like, it's liars and to wait. One of you makes me put up with both and now, I'm going to put an end to it." Somehow, his voice sounds extremely threatening and he turns his head to face me, his blue eyes bore into mine.

"Alex", he says with a mischievous glimpse in his eyes, "your best friend is Lindsey McGordon huh? Red hair, bubbly, talkative per-sonality?"

I don't know what to say, but his face gives out that he already knows the answer and he moves on to Peter.

"And you, Peter", he says empathizing the name, "you're very close to Patricia, your girlfriend you want to keep away from this... business you're in."

Peter clenches his jaw and fists, and I get an extremely uneasy feeling in my stomach.

"Where do you wanna go with this?" Peter asks in a harsh tone.

Zeke cracks into a blinding white smile and I get a feeling that he is no longer my favorite out of my kidnappers.

"Since you guys are very fond of the persons I just named", he starts, "I'm going to use it as an advantage. The rules are simple. Alex, if you're the guilty one, you better tell us now because if you don't, I will bring your friend here as well. Same thing goes for you Peter, if you're the guilty one, you better tell us if you don't want Patricia to know what you've done and what you're doing. If neither of you confesses, I'll just bring both."

I almost choke os the words leave his mouth.

No.

Not Lindsey, he can't do that.

I'm sure my eyes widen to the size of saucers, and I hope it won't give out the fact that I'm the liars.

But if it won't, I still have to confess because I can't be the reason to Lindsey being kidnapped too. It's just... too terrible to even think of.

This time, I'm trapped, because Patricia is my friend too, and even though it would hurt Peter to let her know what he's been doing, I can't risk having her here either.

I glance over at Peter, whose face is now pale as if he's seen a ghost.

My heart is threatening to jump out of my chest or up my throat to choke me to death, and everything starts to spin around and melt into a blur.

The time seems to go in slow-motion and I try to open my mouth to let out the few words that would let them know I'm the liar, but the words get stuck in my throat and won't come out.

Feelings of panic erupt in my stomach as I try to get the words out, but they refuse to be said out loud.

I swallow in an attempt to make it easier for the words to slip out, but still, my lips won't move, won't make a single sound.

If Peter's face is pale, I must look like a doll of porcelain.

It's whizzing in my ear and I try to focus on getting those words out, tell them it was me, but it's like the connection between my body and will have been cut off.

Through my blurry eyes, I can make out Peter's lips moving, but thanks to the sound in my ears that's almost roaring like waterfalls, I can't hear what he says.

But I did read his lips.

And as the fact of what he said sunk in, the whizzing diminished in strength and vanished, and my sight became sharp once again.

I stared at Peter in confusion and surprise with my mouth slightly opened and my lips formed into an 'o'.

"What?", Nick shouts with controlled anger, and my gaze turns towards him. He stares at Peter as well with furrowed eyebrows, clenched jaw, and a tense body.

"It's me", Peter repeats, "I'm the liar."

Chapter 18: The Call

Nick's point of view:

I stare at Peter, my eyes seeing everything in red as the words slip out of his mouth one more time. He's the liar, but why would he lie? Why would he try to kiss Alex when he knows she belongs to me, that she's mine.

I don't understand, but right now I don't care either.

I've never been good at controlling my anger and this time is no exception.

Alex shifts her gaze from Peter to me, then back at Peter with her mouth slightly opened and eyes widened, waiting for the next move.

I rose up from my seat across from Peter and in a few steps, I'm in front of him, clenching my hand into a fist and punching him right across his jaw before he has time to react.

Peter gives out a moan in pain and his hands immediately reach up to his now sore jaw, and Alex flinched at my move but quickly put back her emotionless face again. The sight makes it twitch in the corner of my lips because I know that under that mask, she's afraid. And I like it, I like to know that she is afraid even though she's putting up a damn good act and fight in her attempt of not showing it.

I like the feeling of power it gives me, I like being in control and I want everything to go as I want to and therefore, I'm now literally pissed off on Peter.

He broke our unspoken bro code; never touch someone else's girl.

As I think about it, my gaze turns back to Alex who is watching me intensely.

Damn, she's so hot... and those eyes of hers...

I don't regret taking her, not even for a split second.

She might hate me right now, but the thought entertains me more than it makes me annoyed. I sure do love a good challenge and Alex is certainly giving me one, it's just one thing she doesn't know. I never lose.

If there is something I've learned in life, it's to live it to the fullest and don't look back, and that's exactly what I'm doing. Living to the fullest.

Do I want something, I take it.

Do I want to say something, no matter how inappropriate it might be, I do.

Do I want to hurt someone, like Peter, I'm gladly doing it.

And the greatest of it all? I don't feel any remorse.

As I grew up, I learned to not be sorry, because all it will do is making you feel like crap and acting helpless. You have to fight back and show that you're the one in control, and trust me, that's exactly what I've done. But the past is in the past, no need to bring it up.

I like to live in the moment and in this moment, I want Peter to feel sorry for what he has done. Only because I don't have anything common with remorse, it doesn't mean the people around me feels the same.

And thanks to Zeke, I know the perfect punishment.

"Alex", I called, "go back to our room and stay there, if I find you anywhere else, you'll get punished too, got it?"

I meet her intense stare as she bit her lip and shakes her head.

"No...", she mumbles almost inaudible and I clench my fist even harder, trying to control my anger and annoyance. I do want to release it all, but not on her.

Peter confessed, and that means Alex is innocent, but if I had to put money on who I did think was lying before I knew, my money would have gone on Alex. I mean, her escaping isn't such an unexpected thought, I know she's going to try if she gets the perfect moment, and that's why I'm not going to give it to her.

But Peter, he had sworn he didn't have a thing for Alex, I've made sure to ask him before since he's been a part of us guys for almost three years now, and been hanging out with Alex since she started in his class about a year ago.

I didn't take any notice of her at first when he named her in passing, but as time passed I started to actually listen to what he said about her.

Yeah, he did ask us to specifically not take Alex or anyone else of his so called 'friends' from high school, but he knows as well as all other of us, that if we really want someone, we take her, or him. And I just happened to really want Alex, but she's really getting on my nerves at times, like now.

"What did you say?" I ask her even though I did hear her. I just want her to repeat it, I want to see how far she's willing to go against my will.

She takes a deep breath and gives me a glare, which she immediately wipes away as she remembered what I said about that behavior.

I thought she would shut up to and do as I told her, but no, she holds my gaze and somehow manages to show all the hate and disgust she feels without glaring.

"No", she repeats, this time with a stronger and louder voice, and I groan loudly.

"Fine", I mutter under my breath and look at Zeke, who hasn't said anything in a long time. I still don't trust Alex, and I don't know if she was honest when she came into the living room before and said she wanted to talk to Peter.

"Can you watch her for a while?", I ask him and he gives me a nod and a questioning look.

Before he asks me where I'm going, I answer him.

"I'm going to do a phone call to his little girlfriend if you don't mind?" I know Zeke's the one who makes all decisions, but we're more like brothers than colleagues and as expected, he just gives me a nod and I reaches out my hand towards Peter.

"Your phone, now", I growl, and he looks at me with pleading eyes.

"No, please don't. She doesn't need to kn-"

I snap the phone out of his shaky hand, he knew better than not listening to me with Zeke in the room, so he had reluctantly picked it up from his pocket.

Knowing Peter code, I put in the digits and searched for his girl-friend's name in the contacts. As I do so, he is pleading and begging me not to call her, but I'm not in the mood to listen to him and snaps at him to shut up.

"You know what?" I say as I find her number, "just because you're so annoying, I'm gonna stay here and call her, letting you hear every single word I'm telling her. I wonder what she will think when I tell her about you helped getting one of her friends kidnapped? And since you practically threw yourself over Alex, I'm not going to punish you as much as I would want to." A growing smirk is plastered on my lips and Peter looks at me with widened eyes full of terror.

"What are you going to do?" he breathes out heavily with glossy eyes. Seriously, is he crying?

"Oh, Peter", I almost sing, "I'm not going to punish you for touching my girl because I've realized it would be so much funnier if your own girl took the fall for you."

I smile to myself at the thought of my idea, which I really liked by the way.

"Oh, the irony", I think out loud, "you've told the truth because you didn't want Patricia to get involved, and look where it got you."

Peter is now screaming his lungs out, and I hush him as I look down at the screen to press the green phone icon. Just as I'm about to press call, a high pitched scream tells me to stop. I turn my head towards the source of the screaming and look at Alex as I feel the annoyance grow bigger inside of me.

"And why would I stop?"

Her bottom lip is actually trembling, and she give up her tries of getting out of the grip Zeke's holding her in. I've seen him taking a hold on her shoulders as I took Peter's phone, and I think Alex would have run up to me by now if it wasn't for his grip.

"Because", Alex says in a voice barely above a whisper, "if you bring Patricia here, you won't just hurt Peter, you'll hurt me too. Patricia is my friend. Please, Nick, don't call her. Don't bring her here."

I look at her with a face blank of emotions. As I said before, I don't feel any remorse.

"Sorry Alex", I say without meaning it, "but maybe you have to learn too."

I pressed call and Zeke put a hand over Alex's mouth, suffocating her screams. Patricia can't know Alex's here, not yet. She will just have to see it with her own eyes.

Chapter 19: Promise

✳ back to Alex's pov*

I watch in horror as Nick press the call button, his words ringing in my ear.

Sorry Alex, but maybe you have to learn too.

No, he can't bring Patricia here. She doesn't deserve it, no one does.

The time is ticking in slow motion, but my brain is working ten times faster than usual.

I have to do something, but what?

I can't just let him call her, can I?

Tears are now resting in the brim of my eyes and I've stopped fighting against Zeke's grip.

My eyes wander to Peter, and as I take in his appearance, widen and reddened eyes full of fear, my heart hurts a bit. I don't like Peter because of what he have done, but if I would have confessed and told the truth, I would've been in the exactly same position and state as him.

One look at him, and my walls of self-defense fell.

I bite Zeke's hand, a yelp of pain slipping out of his throat, at the same time the valuable seconds is ticking away.

Zeke reluctantly removes his hand from my mouth for a split second, and before I have time to stop myself, my voice is heard all over the room.

"Stop!"

Nick doesn't even give me a look.

"I'm the real liar, not Peter!" I blurt out, my voice shaking and my chin facing the ceiling as I try to avoid Zeke who is trying to replace his hand over my mouth.

Nick turns around and his dark eyes bore into mine, his grip around the phone tightening causing his knuckles to whiten.

"What?" he spits out with controlled anger and Zeke gives up in his attempt of shut me up. I gulp and look down in my clenched fists.

Was this a good idea? Not at all.

Necessary? Yes.

"Please hung up and I will exp-"

"Explain?", he cuts me off, "I don't think so. You've had your chance."

The clock is running, the seconds ticking away, my brain working at its full speed.

All the feelings I have is tearing me apart from the inside, and the panic is the biggest one.

Nick body suddenly stiffens and realization strikes me with yet another unwelcoming feeling accompanying. Horror.

Patricia picked up. I know she did because Nick's facial features suddenly changed from grimly to concentrated.

As he opens his mouth to answer the light voice which is on the other side of the line, I act, or in this case speak, before thinking.

"I'll do anything!"

I don't understand the power of those words once they are bonded together, let alone do I know that I'll soon find out.

All I know is that those words did catch Nick's attention as he once again turns to face me.

"Anything?" he asks and mutes the phone, his voice somewhat sounding different, "you promise you'll do anything?"

I understand by his tone that he take those words far more important than me, and I start thinking the words through.

Can I really promise him I'll do anything if he hangs up the call? No.

"Maybe not anything...", I trail off and he shakes his head at me.

"Wrong answer, gorgeous."

He turns his back to me and replaces the phone by his ear, unmuting it, and starts talking to the innocent girl on the other line.

"Hello, Patricia. As you hear, this isn't Peter, but one of his friends. Listen, I have something to tell you, but don't ask any questions, okay? It's really important. You know Pe-"

"I promise", I cry out and rush towards Nick to make sure he ends the phone call. As promised, or expected, he does, and I end up half a meter away from him, suddenly not knowing what to do.

"You", Nick says as he takes a step closer and decreases the distance between us, "just saved your friends skin, and turned yourself in."

"No", I say with a harsher tone than expected, "I told you I'll do anything, which isn't the same as turning yourself in. I owe you, nothing more. You better use the favor wisely, but I rather see it as you don't use it at all."

Nick smirks at me and his fingers start follow the outline of my jaw.

"Oh, gorgeous, you can bet I'll use it", he leans in closer, his lips brushing against my ear, "but I'm a patient man, and I will save it for later. And don't worry, I'm standing by my word of not being such a bad guy as you seem to believe."

His words send chillers down my spine, but I feel a minimal amount of relief at his last words.

I back away, and Peter caught my eyes. His lips silently form the words 'thank you' and his eyes are full of joy and relief and I give him a barely noticeable nod in response.

I didn't do it for him.

I did it for myself and my conscience, and for Patricia.

"C'mon, dinner's ready", Zeke sigh and gets up from the couch. I wonder if he had enjoyed the scene of what had just occurred. I certainly didn't because I just realized I've thrown myself head over heels into something I shouldn't have.

Patricia's pov

The phone call abruptly ends and I stare at my phone with furrowed eyebrows.

What had just happened?

Who was that guy I've just spoken to and was he going to tell me something about Peter?

And most important of all, why had I heard Alex's voice shouting in the background?

I can almost swear it was her voice, saying something that sounded like 'I'll do anything'. Her soft voice, and especially the high pitched tone she gets as she raises her voice, isn't something you'll forget in a hurry.

I know I have to tell someone about this, that I'm almost sure of that I've heard Alex, but how will I explain it was through Peter's phone?

Why is Peter's phone at the same place as Alex if he isn't there? What was the guy I talked to going to say? It sounded like he started saying Peter's name.

Does Peter have something to do with Alex's kidnapping?

Nick's pov

I know I just lied to Alex. She promised me she'll do anything if I hung up the phone call, and I did, so it's not actually a lie, but I know she will consider it as one.

I'm not sure, but there's a risk that Peter's girlfriend, Patricia I think, heard Alex as she shouted her little promise, and I don't like taking this kind of risks where I can get caught. Alex and Peter won't like it for sure, but they just have to accept it. It's not like they have any choice.

I'm going to give Patricia a little visit, and I can't promise I will come
back empty handed.

Chapter 20: Difficult

* Alex's pov*

I wake up to the sound of voices shouting, or more like talking in raised voices, and my eyes immediately flickers to the digital clock on the bedside table.

09:28 AM.

I want to get up, but I feel Nick's arms around my waist in a slack grip. If I move, I wake him up, if I don't move, I have to stay in his arms.

When did my life turn into this? My problems changing from not understanding the algebra homework to contemplating whether or not I should get out off a bed I'm sharing with Nick.

Oh, yeah I just remembered. Since Peter stabbed me in the back and I got kidnapped.

As you see, I'm still not over Peter's betrayal but still I did him a favor yesterday.

I still gave Nick a promise and honestly? I'm terrified of what I've got myself into, and what scares me the most is that Nick hasn't said anything more about it.

After the dinner yesterday, we'd gone back to his room but he'd remained silent with only a smirk playing on his lips.

His silence scares me because I know he's mad, furious even, because I lied. But still he hasn't done anything, but I'm just waiting for him to explode. I know he hasn't forgiven me, I know he might burst out on me as soon as I make a wrong move.

He's a ticking time bomb, and might as well explode any second.

That's also the reason to why I decide to stay in bed, even though my brain yells at me to move, because I don't want to anger him, not now.

Does he scare me? Sadly, yes.

Do I like being this close to him? No.

Do I want to get the hell away from him? Absolutely.

Can I do as I want? Nope.

Being kidnapped sucks, being stabbed in the back sucks, not being able to do what you want sucks. Right now, my life sucks, but I won't give up. If you're at the bottom you can only climb higher, right?

"Mhmm", Nick mumbles beside me, and I turn my head slightly to look at him. He is about to wake up, and as he starts moving around a bit his eyes flickers open.

"Good morning, gorgeous", he says in a raspy morning voice and I scoff in response.

"C'mon", he purrs in my ear, "caring enough to give me a morning kiss?"

He tightens his arms around my waist as he said so, pulling me even closer to his bare chest.

"Not really...", I trail off and I feel his chest vibrate as he chuckles.

"It wasn't really an offer you could deny."

With those words, he turns me around and presses his lips onto mine before I have time to do anything - before I have time to react. I don't kiss back, no way, and Nick seems to notice and the kiss turns from soft to hard, more demanding and harsh.

As he licks my bottom lip, asking for entrance, I use all my strength to push him off of me, and his lips separate from mine.

"Why?", I whine like a little kid, "I didn't say or do anything wrong!"

"No, you didn't", Nick says in a soft voice and brings me back into his arms, "but you just look too damn adorable I couldn't stop myself."

I feel my cheeks becoming heated and I'm actually glad that I'm facing his chest right now because I don't want him to see me blush. In fact, I don't want to blush at all. This was the first time he said something you can associate with cute, but then I remember; nothing's cute with Nick.

"We better get up now, gorgeous. We got a long day in front of us."

I furrow my eyebrows in confusion even though he can't see.

"Doing what?", I mutter into his chest, "playing video games?"

He chuckles again and pulls me back a bit so that my face is facing his.

"No", he smiles, "you, my princess, are going to hang out with Danny, Vince, and Will today. Oh, and their girls."

I'm still looking like a question mark and I bit my bottom lip as I'm contemplating whether or not to ask him why. I decide to do it.

"Why? Why with them? And who is Danny? And what are you going to do? And why the new pet name?" Dealing with one possessive, maniac kidnapper is one thing, but dealing with three? I don't know how I will handle it. And seriously? Doesn't he think one awful pet name is enough?

"Aw", Nick teases, "you want me to be there with you, how sweet. And for your other questions, Danny is just one of 'us', I wanted to try out a new pet name but don't worry, I definitely going to stick with gorgeous, and I'm not going to be with you today because I'm going out on a ... field trip."

I eye him suspiciously. "What kind of field trip?"

"Nothing special", he shrugs, "don't worry about me, gorgeous. You're going to be busy enough worrying about yourself." I open my mouth to ask him what he means, but he puts a finger to my lips to hush me.

"Just go and get ready."

An hour later, I'm standing in Nick's room again with my arms crossed over my chest.

"Nu-uh, I'm not going to wear that", I protest and shakes my head.

We've just got back from the breakfast and Nick is holding a pair of clothes for me to take and change into, but I refuse.

"You can barely call that for shorts", I point out", and that's just a sports bra. At least give me decent clothes of I have to be stuck with three hooligans for the day."

Nick groans in frustration and runs a hand through his hair.

"C'mon, do you have to be this difficult?"

I raise my eyebrows at him. "Yes, I do."

He let his hand fall from his hair and his facial expression suddenly changes, and not for the better. Uh oh.

"I don't like your attitude, don't you remember the rules?", he says and speaks painfully slow. I feel my cheeks heat and I stumble as I search for the right words.

"I-I'm... Y-you..."

"What did you say?", he jeers, placing his hand behind his ear as if he couldn't hear me.

I bit my lips to prevent myself from giving a witty comeback.

"Huh?"

"Nothing", I mutter and his lips curls upwards in a sneer.

"That's what I thought, now go and put this on."

Reluctantly, I take the revealing clothes and lock myself in the bathroom.

I quickly change and takes a skeptical look in the mirror and immediately shakes my head, causing my hair to dance around my face.

No way I'm wearing this.

I search around the room as Nick pounds on the door, telling me to hurry up, and my eyes land on the hamper.

I dig it through, even though it might be disgusting, until I find a big shirt with a print of the reaper on it.

This will do, I tell myself with a shrug and put it over my 'clothes'.

"What the hell?" Nick shouts as I step out, "you really never give up, huh?"

I shrug in response, not wanting to anger him by saying something.

"Whatever", he mutters after a while, "but just this one time because I won't be here, got it?"

I give him a small nod, and he grabs my arm and drags my out of the room, through a corridor into another until we stop in front of a door, which I haven't set my foot inside.

As he opens it, he pushes me in before slamming it shut behind me and I realize he didn't follow. He left me, and I slowly turn my face to the rest of the room and six pairs of eyes are staring at me.

I realize I'm in a gym room and I recognize two of the girls as Amy, who I've seen before, and the girl who's in the year above me, I can't remember her name.

Will, the one who sprained my ankle, has his arms around Amy, who's looking terrified, and the other girl I recognize stand with the arms of a brown haired, brown eyed guy around her. The last girl, who I don't know, has blonde, shoulder-length hair and big green eyes widened in fear and, of course, Vince's arm around her waist.

"Okay", Vince speaks up and pushes the girl away from him, under other circumstances it would've looked funny, but now it didn't.

"Since everyone's here now, we should get started", Vince continues with a smirk, "We, Danny, Will and I, are going to see what you girls got. We're going to check your fighting skills, strength, and stamina. And you girls ain't gonna stop until we tell you to. Got it?"

I see the three other girls nod as I just stay on my ground, and Vince looks at me with raised eyebrows. He takes a few steps closer until he is standing right in front of me, our faces inches apart.

"Did you not hear me?" he groans, clearly annoyed, "I said, got it?"

I don't want him to get the pleasure to see my fear, so I hide in and stare him right in the eyes.

"Yes", I say sternly, "I got it. I'm not deaf."

"She got quite an attitude", the brown haired and brown eyed guy chuckles from behind Vince, who turns around with anger showing in his blue-grey eyes.

"Shut up, Danny", he spits and turns his gaze back at me. "We're going to start with the fighting, and you're up first."

I keep my head high, even though his words increased my fear, and I even curl up my lips into a small smirk.

"And whose ass am I going to kick?"

Now, Vince smiles crookedly. "You're going to race against me, but sorry to break it to you, hun, but you're the one who's going to get your ass kicked."

I gulp, feeling my confidence wash off of me.

I'm going to get my ass kicked.

Chapter 21: Fingers Crossed

Three seconds. Three seconds was all it took before I was laying down with my face pressed against the floor with Vince on top of me.

Oh, the joy of feeling your confidence wash off of you in a matter of seconds is just beautiful, isn't it? I hope you noticed the sarcasm.

"Not so cocky anymore, huh?" he taunts and I groan in pain.

"C'mon, Vince", Danny pleads and my liking towards him immediately grows. But not enough for me to not hate him, I just don't hate him as much as the others.

"Not until she's begging for it herself", Vince spit and my body tense.

No way. I'm not going to sink that low. I'm not going to humiliate myself.

"I'm wait-", he starts but gets interrupted as the door slams open.

"Well, well, well..." the newly arrived person mocks, "stuck in a sticky situation, buttercup?"

Oh no. The stupid pet name, buttercup. I only know one person who called me that, and I easily puzzle the pieces together.

What was his name again, Kirk?

I turn my head towards the door and another groan of frustration escapes my lips as I see the slightly familiar face, which indeed belongs to Kirk.

"I didn't think you would be here today, man", Will greets him and do this weird handshake and hug I've never learned nor understood.

"I wasn't planning to", Kirk answers and flashes me an evil smirk. I hate making fun of myself and let me tell you, these guys seems to love it.

"Just let me go", I mutter under my breath, "it wasn't a fair play."

Vince chuckles from on top of me.

"Oh, really? And why not?"

I know that what I'm going to say sounds silly, but at this moment, silly is all I got.

"I wasn't ready..."

My words cause everyone in the room to laugh, except for the girls who still have scared expressions on their pale faces.

"So you think you can beat me?", Vince taunts and I decide to let my old, or more like real, self come out.

"I know I can", I say confidently, "if we're going to play by your rules, I'm sure of it."

"My rules?" he questions and a small smile starts tugging in the corner of my lips, but sadly, or maybe fortunately, Vince can't see it.

"Yeah", I state, "your rules. And if your brain can't take in what I'm saying, which is understandable considering how much bullshit it's full of, you just have to wait and see what I mean. But I would appreciate it if you could get your disgusting hands and body off of me."

He scoffs in response, but loosens his grip on my hand and thankfully gets off of me.

"We'll see about that", he says in a warning tone, "but now I think it's time for all of you girl to show us what you got."

And then, the hell consisting of hours of training started.

An eternity later, at least it's what it felt like, Vince told us we were done and all of us immediately stopped with whatever we were doing.

I quickly got off the treadmill I've been using for the past half an hour and put on an exhausted mask. Surely, I was tired, but it was now time for my act of revenge to start.

Remember when I told Vince I knew I could beat him? Well, it's time now. He doesn't pay any more attention towards me than any other of the girls and I doubt that he even remembers what I've told him a few hours ago.

I walk towards him, breathing heavily and deliberately walking with my head bowed down. As I'm right in front of him, I stop and place my hands on my knees, pretending to take deep breaths.

"Aw, already tired?" Vince mocks and I can feel his warm breath against my neck.

He has leaned in closer and a smile is tugging at the corner of my lips.

Time for action.

I quickly turn my face up to face Vince, a smirk is plastered on his lips but as I place my hands on his shoulders and knees him in the crotch, faster than he can comprehend, I see his face twist in pain and his eyes filling with surprise, pain, and anger.

"You little bi-", he curses but before he has time to fulfill the sentence, my clenched fist connects with his jaw.

I admit, he's not the only one who got hurt by the punch, but it's definitely worth it.

Vince stumbles backward, but I follow his every move and punch him again, and again, until someone suddenly grabbed a hold of me from behind and dragged me away from Vince, who is now bloody and literally pissed off.

"Let me go!", I yell at the one who is holding me back, and as I throw a glance behind me I recognize it as Danny, whose jaw is clenched and brown hair unwittingly messed up.

Will and Kirk, however, are holding Vince back. Vince's eyes are burning with anger, his muscles are tensed as he tries to push Will and Kirk off of him and get to me, but thankfully he doesn't succeed.

Danny pushes me down on a weight bench, and I'm not stupid enough to stand up in an attempt of running away. Instead, I cross my arms in front of my chest and glare at him but I can't hold back the small smile on my lips as I see Vince, all bloody, on the other side of the room.

"You know he is gonna get back at you, right?" Danny sighs and I nod.

"Yeah, if Nick will let him." I know I can't use Nick as my safe card but right now I don't care about the consequences, it felt good to hit Vince. It felt good to wipe the smile off his lips.

"I gotta admire your courage", Danny says as he shakes his head, "but what you did was just plain stupid."

I shrug at his words and restlessly pull my hair out of the ponytail I put it in and starts twirling my fingers around a few strands.

During the past few hours, I've learned the name of all the girls and I watch them with a sad expression. They seems to be terrified, not that I'm not because I am, but fear is all they are showing and as soon as one of the guys even glance at them, they flinch.

I've learned that the girl who's from the year above me in school is named Nicole. She's tall, with light eyelashes, natural red hair, and freckled face, and the scared expression she wears doesn't suit her at all. Her widened gray eyes should show happiness and not fear, no one of these girls should be scared, but being here can probably break even the strongest one. I just hope I'm not next, I just hope that the 'can probably' isn't true, and I really hope we're getting out of here soon, me and the girls.

I've been here in a few days, and it's the living hell. Imagine how it must feel after nearly a month, because that's how long Aubrey, the short-haired blonde girl, has been here.

If you think it will get better the longer you're stuck here, you're wrong. At least that's what Aubrey told me the few minutes during our training that we managed to get close enough to talk without the guys noticing. Sadly, she was the only one I managed to talk to, because as we got caught, I don't think any other of the girls even dared to breathe properly, afraid that it would make too much sound.

"Okay, time to go and change!" Will yells and I realize that Vince is no longer in the room. I've been too caught up in my thoughts to realize he left.

Kirk approaches me and I raise my eyebrows at him.

"I'm your escort", he smirks and I scoff in response but do follow him back to Nick's room. As he opens the door to the bedroom, Kirk gives me a small push and closes the door behind me without following me in. I hear the lock twist and know for sure that I'm, once again, stuck in Nick's room.

I sigh loudly and takes off the trainers Nick gave me before he left, and then I head into the bathroom and jump into the shower once I dumped my sweaty clothes in the hamper.

I take my time in the shower, just relaxing and welcoming the hot water that washes over my body and tense muscles, and I don't step out until the water runs cold.

I quickly dry myself and wrap a towel around my body, and it's not until now I realize I didn't take any clothes with me inside.

I groan slightly and let out a few curses and slowly walks towards the door. I should still be alone, right?

As I open the door, instantly being hit by the cold air, I realize I'm wrong.

"Hello, gorgeous", Nick welcomes, "you certainly took your time in there."

I give him a glare before I manage to stop myself.

"I need clothes", I say and as I try to hide behind the door, but of course, Nick has to ruin it all by stepping towards me and push the door wide open.

"You don't really need them..." he says slowly as his eyes trail down my body. He moistens his lips as he looks back at my face, his gaze laying a few more seconds on my lips.

If he thinks he can kiss me, he's wrong.

"I do need them", I state and tries to not show any emotions at all and he chuckles.

"Fine, you'll get them on one condition."

I I eye him suspiciously, knowing that nothing good can come out of what he just said.

"What condition?"

"Kiss me", he starts and hushes me as I open my mouth to tell him no way, "or... you can put both of your hands up on three."

I drop my jaw at his words, my lips forming into a small 'o', and a disgusted sound makes its way out of my throat as I realize what he means, or more like what he wants out of the second action he named.

"You're such a perv-", I cry but he puts his finger to my lips to hush me.

"Sch, don't want to get punished now, do we?" He pulls up his lips into a crooked smirk, or more like a sneer, and I bite my own lip to not talk back.

"Damn... you look good when you do that", he says in a breath and I give him a questioning look.

"Doing what?" I try to remain calm, with my emotionless mask on, but I'm honestly feeling extremely uncomfortable and terrified. I'm just wearing a towel for freaking sake!

"Biting your lip." I immediately stop tugging at it and he chuckles at my reaction.

"So what's it gonna be?" he asks and I shake my head.

"Neither." How easily manipulated do he think I am?

He then pushes me against the wall, resting his arms on both sides of me head, trapping me.

"Gorgeous, you know that's not the right answer. Alternative one or two?"

I know that my next move is going to be the most childish ever, but if he buys it, I don't care.

"You know what?" I say with a light tone, not sounding like me at all, it sounds way too happy, "if you give me some clothes now, I promise I will kiss you as I've changed. And not just a simple kiss, if you're nice I might as well give you a full make out session.

Nick does honestly look completely surprised over what I just said, and I can't really blame him. His eyes lit up, the smirk on his face grew bigger, but then he suddenly furrows his eyebrow and looks at my suspiciously.

"You promise? And why not right now?" He questions, tilting his head slightly.

I give him an attempt of a faked smile, as if I'm shy or uncomfortable. "I promise", I say, fingers crossed behind my back, "and I don't trust you, and therefore I don't want to kiss you in only a towel."

His smirk grows even bigger if possible, and his eyes lit up with something I can't point out.

"Alright", he says and backs off, grabbing a bunch of clothes laying on the bed. I practically rip the clothes from his hands and take a hold onto the doorknob, making sure of that my towel won't fall down.

"Oh, and Nick?" I'm almost singing with joy and he turns his attention towards me. I show him my crossed fingers and flashes him a genuine smile.

"Sorry to break it to you, but fingers crossed, I lied."

I quickly slam the door shut, giggling at his shocked expression. He starts banging on the door, pounding on it with his fists.

"C'mon, Alex!" he shouts, calling me by my normal nickname for once, "open the damn door!"

I quickly put on the clothes he gave me, which were one of his shirts - surprise, surprise- and a pair of legging, plus the undergarment.

Contemplating on whether or not I should open the door, I decide to do it, not wanting to risk getting into serious trouble.

Nick gives me a look of mixed feelings. Irritation, for lying to him, and amusement and joy by seeing me in his clothes, which I for the record don't like.

You can borrow a shirt from a boyfriend, not a kidnapper.

"Alex, Alex, Alex...", he sighs as if he's a disappointed teacher or parent, "what shall I do with you? You're lying, you're sarcastic, arrogant... You're not treating me with respect... And you never seem to learn."

I bite my lip and look at him, not caring what he thinks about. "Oh, I do actually learn, I just don't care about what you're saying. I'm a living creature, not a pet."

He smiles mischievously at me.

"Oh, I know, gorgeous, and you wanna know how? Because you're mine. You're not my pet, you're my girl, you're my Alex."

I'm just about to reply with a sentence full of curses when a scream pierces through the air. Not a scream of pain; a scream of fear. And I know the voice because I've heard it so many times before.

Patricia.

My eyes dart at Nick. "What did you do?" I yell at him. He looks at me with a hard and slightly confused expression.

"What do you mean?"

"What did you do when you were out?", I scream, starting to breathe heavily.

Nick decides to play stupid.

"Out?"

I can feel tears threaten to fall down my cheeks.

"You said you were going on a field trip", I say with a shaky voice, "what did you do?"

I can see his jaw clench, and his whole body tense up.

"That's none of you busine-"

He gets cut off by another scream, this one formed into words.

"Let go of me! Help!"

I clench my hands into a fist and stare at Nick with hatred in my eyes.

"Why is Patricia here?" I yell, close to losing control, "you kidnapped her. Why? You promised you wouldn't! You lied, you... you're son of a-"

He puts a hand over my mouth to silence me, pressing his body against mine as he does so.

At the moment, I'm not in the mood to do as he wants and I bite his hand and he hisses in pain and takes it off of my mouth.

I push him away and starts pounding at his chest, screaming and crying at the same time.

He kidnapped Patricia.

One of my friends, who he promised not to take.

He lied, he can't be trusted.

He is a bad guy, he doesn't have any feelings at all.

He is a monster.

"Alex, Alex!" Nick tries to get my attention, and he takes a hold onto my wrist, preventing me from pounding on his chest and I start kicking him instead.

"For freaking sake, Alex! Sto-"

I knee him in the crotch, and he lets out his breath and a sound of intense pain. I take the change and get out of his loosening grip, and run towards the door.

Maybe it wasn't locked now when he is in the room too.

I turn the doorknob.

I was right, it wasn't locked.

Nick calls on me to get back, but I ignore him and starts sprinting towards the stairs. I know I probably won't get out, but that's not my plan. My plan is to see Patricia.

Luckily, I don't meet anyone as I reach the stairs and I sprint up to the main floor, towards the living room.

As I reach it, I stop dead in my tracks.

A blonde girl is forced down on her knees on the floor, with a gun pressed against her temple.

The one who is holding it is Vince. My hatred towards him doesn't seem to stop, ever. It just increases for every time I see him.

"What the hell?" Kirk, who is standing aside watching, says.

Vince darts his eyes towards me. Zeke and Will, who are standing aside watching as well, both look at me. Patricia, who has her head bowed down and is crying for her life, darts her reddened eyes at me. Everyone's eyes are on me, and I suddenly feel extremely self-conscious.

"A-alex?" Patricia stutters and I rush forward to her, but someone sneaks their arms around my waist and drags me back. My fingers brush against Patricia's, whose hands are reaching for me. I try to squirm out of the grip and get to Patricia and tell her everything is going to be okay, but I can't. The grip around me only tightens and drags me away from Patricia, and I scream after her.

"Patricia!"

And she calls back; "Alex!"

"Let me go!" I yell at the person who is dragging me away. I'm almost out of the room by now, and my vision is blinded by tears.

"Relax. Seriously, Alex, they aren't gonna shoot her", Nick whispers in my ear, which only makes me even crazier.

"You did this!" I shout at him, my voice high-pitched and full of pain, "you bastard! Let her go! She has nothing to do with this. You promised, Nick... Let her go!"

"I'm sorry", he whispers, his warm breath hitting my neck, "but I can't do that."

I know his words are meaningless, there's no truth behind them. For him, sorry is just a word he says when it fits, but he doesn't know what it means. For Nick, sorry is just a word without meaning, a word as empty as his heart.

Chapter 22: Monster

I hate him. I hate him so much, words can't even describe it.

You know when you're in school and have this really annoying teacher who you says you hate?

That teacher would look like an angel beside Nick.

If I wasn't sure if he was the devil in disguise before, I sure as hell am now.

The thought of what he's done makes me sick. It makes me want to puke.

I thought there was something good inside of him but apparently, I was wrong.

How could I even think that? I mean, the list of what he's done is pretty long.

He kidnapped me.

He gave me a stupid pet name.

He forcefully kisses me and let's not talk about how he seems to love to nibble on my earlobe and caress my arms and cheeks.

He talks about how he will enjoy breaking me.

He doesn't feel any remorse.

He kidnaps people for money, and he's okay with it.

He promised to not bring Patricia to this hell hole.

He broke his promise.

How on earth could I not see that coming?

Right now, I'm clenching my fist only to unclench it the moment after, over and over again to resist the urge to choke Nick. Which I know I can't even do.

The world is unfair, and I hate it.

My vision is blinded by hate, all I'm seeing goes in red. I'm fuming and I wouldn't be too surprised if there would start to come out steam out of my ears.

Nick had dragged me back downstairs, but he didn't put me in his own room, no he had to throw me in a small room which looks more like a cell than a real room.

The walls are gray without any paint on them, and the only furniture in the room is a couch, except for the old lamp which casts a yellow light over this incredibly small room.

If I would be claustrophobic, I can tell you that I would've gone crazy by now. There's no windows in the room, no pictures on the wall. Nothing.

If I stretch out my arms, standing in the middle of the room, I can touch the walls on both sides of me. That's how small it is and it's about twice as long as wide.

Even though I'm not claustrophobic, I can feel my breathing getting heavier. I've been here for at least half an hour now, and my knuckles are red and bloody from all the pounding I've done on the door, and my throat hurt from all the screaming I did the first ten minutes after

Nick put me in here. I didn't scream or pound on the door out of fear of this room, no I did it because of how angry I was, and I still am.

Luckily for Nick, I can't do much in here but if he would've thrown me in his own room, I can tell you it would've been trashed by now.

I'm not the one to break down in anger, losing control, but I guess being here have changed that. Being here have changed me.

I didn't be like this before, I didn't use to be full of hate and fear and always come back with witty, sarcastic comments. That side of me did I only bring out when someone really did piss me off or annoy me. I saved it to those who deserved it, and I guess those ones are in this building right now. Or I don't even guess, I know.

A light knock on the door draws me back to reality and I get up from the surprisingly comfortable couch I've placed myself in as I gave up on getting out.

"Calmed down enough to think clearly yet?" Nick asks as the door unlocks and opens.

"Where is she?" I growl, ignoring his question and trying to push myself past him through the doorway.

He grabs my by my shoulders and looks me straight in the eyes.

"Alex, calm down", he says sternly, "she's okay."

I'm extremely close to spitting him right in the face, but my common sense stops me in the last second.

"I don't believe you, and I want to see her", I state but Nick shakes his head, making me even angrier.

"Sorry, but I don't think it's got for either of you. You know she did freak out even more as she saw you, huh?"

My eyes turn black as I look at him, my jaw and fist clenching.

"What was I supposed to do?" I ask him. "Just sit back, relax and shrug it off? Ignoring that you broke your promise and brought one of my closest friends here?"

"No, that's not what I meant", he sighs and pinches the bridge of his nose in frustration. "Just leave it now, Alex. Please? I don't want to keep you in here but if you don't calm down you'll leave me with no choice."

I'm trying my best not to cry in front of him, I don't want to cry at all but it's hard. It's hard because my life has taken such a fatal turn in a matter of days.

I force myself to take deep breaths, calming myself down, but I'm not doing it for Nick, I'm doing it for myself.

The clock is ticking, for what I don't know, but after a while, I've calmed myself down.

"Ready to get out if this room?" he asks me and I nod and let him lead me out. As the door slam shut behind us I turn around to face him with pleading eyes.

"Please let me see her! Please..."

Once again, he shakes his head in response and gives me a gentle but firm push in the direction of his room.

"No can do, sweetheart", he says in a smooth voice, trying out a new pet name at the same time.

I don't give up that easily, and turn around again, this time with my eyes even bigger and pounding lips, with a quivering bottom lip.

He looks at my lips for a few seconds, being completely silent, and then suddenly press me against the wall, trapping me with his body.

Nick takes a soft but firm grip around my chin, forcing me to look up at him and then, without me being able to react or stop him, he crashes his lips onto mine. As I take in what he's doing, I try to get him off of me but it's of no use. My arms are pinned down by his own, and as soon as I move my head to break the kiss, he follows my motion, keeping it going.

The painfully slow seconds it takes before he finally breaks it off because of lack of oxygen, I feel my cheeks turn a shade of red. It's not because of that I'm embarrassed, no it's because I'm mad.

As he takes his awful, disgusting lips off of mine, I stare at him with hatred.

"What the hell was that for?" I yell at him and he smirks.

"You practically asked for it, gorgeous", he says, giving me my old pet name back. "You looked at me with those beautiful blue eyes of yours and pouted with your perfectly kissable lips. I just couldn't resist."

He lets me go and I immediately reaches for my lips, wiping them off with the back of my hand with a disgusted facial expression.

Nick chuckles at my reaction and raises an eyebrow.

"You're just silly, gorgeous. The sooner you admit you enjoy kissing me and starts kissing back, the better."

I almost gag at his words and stare at him widened eyed before he takes a step back and drags me with, leading me back to his room in silence.

As we enter, he locks the door -surprise surprise - and I throw myself at the sofa and curl myself into a ball.

"Gorgeous?" he asks but I don't answer.

"Alex?" I still ignore him.

"Allie?" I almost flinch and snap my head up, but I manage not to.

I feel the cushions sink down as he sits down beside me, throwing an arm around me and pulling me close to his chest.

I feel him caress my hair and arm, but I remain emotionless and don't move at all.

"C'mon, Alex. Don't give me the silent treatment."

He kisses me softly on top of my head and sighs loudly.

We sit as that for a few minutes, he with his arms around me as my head is resting against his chest. If he was my boyfriend or just a simple friend, I would've found it soothing, but now I don't. Now, I hate every second of it and suffer in silence.

"Please", he says after countless minutes, "say something, anything."

I close my eyes for a few seconds, breathing in the scent of his cologne.

"I hate you", I whisper, feeling his body tense up at my words, "I hate you, and there's nothing you can do to change it. You're a monster."

Chapter 23: Decent Kisser

A lex's pov

"You coming?" Nick asks me, and I shake my head, causing my hair to dance around my face. I'm sitting on the couch in his room, where I also slept since I was, and still am, frustrated and angry that he brought Patricia here yesterday.

It's about lunchtime, and I already refused eating breakfast and now he is heading off to the kitchen, but I refuse to come with him.

"I change the sentence. You're coming with me, now." He storms over to me and takes a firm grip on my upper arm, and a yelp of pain escapes my throat.

"Ouch! Let go of me you idiot!" I fight against his grip but he refuses to release it.

"Don't use that tone towards me, gorgeous. You're seriously starting to go on my nerves."

I dig my nails from my free hand into the one he's holding me with, and he clenches his fist in anger and pain.

"Stop doing that!" he hisses and as I don't, he suddenly stops dead in his track and turns towards me, placing his hands on my shoulders and pushing me against the wall.

"I said don't", he whispers threateningly in my ear, his breath panting my neck and raising goosebumps on my skin.

"You're either coming with my willingly or not, but you can't escape or disrespect me."

"A little too late for that now, isn't it?" I sigh as I try to control my anger. I know I shouldn't anger him but I just don't seem to be able to stop. I need to push down my button that will make me stop, but I can't seem to find it.

"Gorgeous, gorgeous, gorgeous...", he whispers, "you never seems to learn, do you? You know the punishment-"

"And I don't care about it anymore", I cut him off, and he honestly seem to be surprised and I decide to continue.

"I don't care about if you kiss me, it sure as hell is disgusting but I don't care anymore because there is no possible way you can make me hate you even more than I already do."

His eyes turn dark and he clenches his jaw but then he suddenly moistens his lips and I scream no on the inside as I understand what he's about to do, and I'm right.

Seconds later, he presses his soft lips against mine and I stay completely still but I have to confess something. I lied when I said that I don't care about him kissing me anymore, I still hate it - extremely much.

Sure, he's a decent kisser but that doesn't matter. I still hate him.

He pulls back, his lips separating from mine, and a big smirk forms on his lips.

"You know...", he says in a sinister tone, "if you really don't mind about me kissing you, you might as well kiss back."

Euw.

No.

Never.

"And why would I give you that pleasure?" I ask him. "You won't even let me see Patricia, so why would I give you something you want when I don't get anything in return?"

I expect the smirk to wash off of his face, but it remains.

"Deal", he says and surprises me. "If you kiss me back, and it gotta be extremely good then, I let you see Patricia."

My mind tells me no, or more like screams it, but my lips slowly part and I find myself nodding. Nick sneers and decreases the space between us once again, his hand cups gently around my chin and the other one slips around my waist, and I reluctantly slide my arms around his neck.

His lips connect with mine once again, and this time, I respond to his eager kiss.

It's not nice neither gentle, but harsh and full of lust.

Our lips move in sync and he presses me even closer to his body, his heat radiating off on me. He somehow makes me nearly lose my balance which causes me to bring my legs around him too, and right now he and the wall is the only thing holding me up.

My legs are around his waist, my hands holding onto his shirt and hair, and he is now supporting me with both of his hands.

His tongue licks my bottom lip, asking for entrance, but I refuse and he groans in displeasure and starts nibble on it instead, increasing the strength in his bite until I finally gasp of pain and gives him a chance to slip in. A chance which he takes, and his tongue explored my whole mouth and plays with mine, and behind closed eyelids, my thoughts are begging for it to be over soon. Someone seems to have heard my prayers because, a few seconds later, Nick finally pulls away, gasping for air.

I cough loudly to catch his attention, and then gestures for him to place me down. I don't like the place where his hands are placed to keep my body up, and he puts me down painfully slow.

"Gorgeous", he breaths, "you're absolutely amazing."

I shrug at his words. "Yeah, whatever, remember our deal?"

Nick smirks, placing his arm over my shoulder to keep me close.

"Yes, and I won't break this one, you've deserved it", he winks at me, "let's go and meet Patricia then, but I would want another one of these... make-out sessions when we get back."

Ha, in his dreams.

Chapter 24: Visit

P atricia's pov

flashback

"Lindsey, hang on a sec I'm just gonna go get some water", I tell her through the phone I have pressed between my ear and shoulder as I'm finishing my math homework at the same time.

I justed to do the homework together with Alex, we both used to complain about how utterly stupid it was and that we didn't understand a thing, and then it would always end with us sitting in front of the tv or going out. But now she's not here and I really do miss her.

And I still haven't forgotten about the phone call. I can almost swear that I heard Alex screaming but that would mean Peter has something to do with it but I haven't had the chance to ask him.

I sigh in frustration as I throw the phone on my bed and walk down the stairs to my kitchen. I'm home alone, my mom and dad are over to my grandma with my little brother, but I've decided to stay home.

The sun is shining outside but it still doesn't seem to lighten up my mood. It feels like dark clouds surround me, and I know it's because of Alex and the lack of answers I have to the questions about her. Lindsey's worried too, or more like terrified, and she's honestly a wreck right now, spending all her time thinking about her best friend.

As I pour myself a glass of water and slowly sip the ice cold water, my eyes fill with tears. Everything has changed, and not for the better, and the worst part is that Alex isn't the only one who's missing, kidnapped. Other girls are with her, at least I think so, and I can't even imagine how scared the must be.

With my mood suddenly at its worst, I start walking back towards my room with the glass in my hand.

My foot rest at the first step of the staircase as I hear a light knock on the door and I furrow my eyebrows in confusion.

I didn't expect company.

Still with the glass in my hand, I slowly peek through the peephole in the door only to see a complete stranger standing outside.

He has dark hair and honestly, he looks intimidating.

I take a deep breath and open the door slightly, peeking out.

"Yes?" I ask the guy standing outside, not caring about my surly voice.

"Yeah, hey", he says awkwardly and his voice sounds strangely familiar, "I know this is going to sound real my car broke down and I wonder if I could borrow your phone to call a mechanic?"

I eye him suspiciously and tries to figure out where I could've heard his voice before.

"Why don't you use your own phone?" I ask.

"I didn't have the number", he answers bluntly and I raise my eyebrows at him.

"You could have searched it up."

"I don't have any internet on my phone."

Suddenly, the blood in my veins freezes and my eyes widen. His voice. I know where it comes from. He's the one who talked on the phone when someone called me from Peter's phone. He could have something to do with Alex's kidnapping.

"S-sorry", I stutter, "but I'm really busy right now. You should try another neighbor, I'm sure they're willing to help." As I speak, his eyes turn from light to dark in a matter of seconds and if I thought he looked intimidating before, he looks deadly scary right now.

I try to slam the door shut, but he put his foot in the gap to stop me, and then he grabs the door handle and rips it open. I scream, drop the glass of water to the floor where it shatters into a thousand of pieces, and then run towards the stairs.

My steps are heavy, and I can hear him, the guy, running after me as I aim for the bathroom, screaming at the top of my lungs.

My fingertips brush against the cold handle as my whole body flung forwards, hitting the hard wooden door with as much force that I groan in pain and would have fallen to the ground if it wasn't for the body that holds me up.

"Patricia, Patricia, Patricia...", the guy taunts, "what have your parents told you about letting strangers into your house?"

I'm terrified and my heart is beating at an extremely fast pace in my chest, but then I suddenly remember the phone call I'm currently having with Lindsey. She must have heard me scream, and the door leading into my room is barely two meters away from me, which means she can still hear me.

"W-who are you?" I stutter, desperate for an answer. If he is going to kill me or kidnap me or who knows what, I might as well try to get some answers out of him. He doesn't know about the phone call, and I'm going to use it to my advantage.

"I'm Nick", he says flatly, "but my name would be the least of your worries."

Ignoring the fear that holds me in a firm grip, I decide to take a chance and tell him what I know, or at least what I hope I know. If I'm wrong, if he doesn't have anything to do with Alex's disappearance, I don't know what to say. But if he doesn't, then why would he be here?

"I know what you've done", I say in a raised voice to make sure that Lindsey hears too, and I know for a fact that she never hangs up on the phone, no matter how long you might be gone.

"You're one of the sick maniacs who kidnapped Alex."

He gives out a dark chuckle which sends shivers down my spine.

"Aren't you a smart little girl?" he mocks. "Too bad you won't have any use of it, cause I can't have you running around freely for just the reason you named, honey. You know too much, and I can't risk getting caught, can I?"

"What have you done to her?" I scream, "And what does Peter have to do with it? I know he is involved, you called me from his phone. Is he like you?"

"Like me?", Nick ask even though he doesn't wait for a reply, "no, being like me is a compliment no one deserves to get, but I think you want to know if he is involved and if so, willingly? I gladly tell you the answer is yes. Your boyfriend helped me and the other guys kidnap the gorgeous Alex and the other girls, it's all thanks to him we succeeded."

My heart cracks at his words, and an indescribable pain fills it. No, he can't have... I want to ask more questions about Peter, but I remind myself that I need to give Lindsey as much information as possible so that she can tell it all to the police.

"What other guys? And what are you going to do with me?!"

"You ask too much, Patricia. I'm afraid that I have to shut you up."

I struggle against his grip, even though I know it's useless since that's all I've been doing for the last minute.

"What are you going to do with me? Kill me? Kidnap me like you did with the others?"

"I was thinking about just kidnap you and keep you hostage for a while, but you're so damn annoying I'm contemplating on putting you on the market instead."

"Market?" I shriek without being able to hold back the fear in my voice.

"Yes, the black market", Nick sighs, "you know where you can sell and buy illegal things? We're going to sell a girl at the market next week if her parents don't pay the ransom money, maybe I'll put you there too."

"No, no you can't! Let me go! Let all the girls go! You can't do it, you don't have the right too." I'm now crying, the tears cascading down my face. I'm not strong enough to keep my head up high anymore, the fear is taking over, and I keep screaming at the top of my lungs and fighting against Nick's grip until I feel a sting in my arm, and almost immediately my muscles stop working, becomes limp, and darkness

overcomes me.

Chapter 25: Like A School Play

Alex's pov

Nick lead me to where the room Patricia is held. It's another room in the basement I haven't paid attention to, it's not like he lets me do whatever I want in here, and I impatiently bite my bottom lip and twirl a curl of dark hair between my fingers as Nick search for the right key.

He takes his time and I start thinking he deliberately take as much time as possible to find the right key and putting it in the keyhole. but as he finally does, my patient's almost gone.

I practically throw myself at the door as he put his hand on the doorknob to open it, but he catches a hold of my waist with his other hand and pulls me close to his warm body.

"Take it easy, gorgeous. It's not like she's going to walk away or something", he smirks and I give him a glare, which he immediately respond to by pecking my lips, and my face shows pure disgust for a moment before I manage to put my mask back on. He can't know I'm more affected by it than he thinks, because then he will just continue doing it, and I don't know how much of it I can take without throwing up.

He flashes me another smirk and opens the door. I want to rush inside, hug Patricia and just comfort her, be here for her, but Nick holds me back.

The room is pretty small, with a mattress with a pillow and a blanket in one of the corners, an armchair, and a small shelf filled with a couple of books. The wall is a dull yellow shade and the only thing that lightens up the room is a lamp that's connected to the wall, and my sympathy for Patricia increases.

I try to get out if Nick's grip as he turns most of his attention to the door as he locks it from the inside, but I fail and he raises his eyebrows at me.

"Please?" I beg, tears filling my eyes. I'm crying to get what I want, not because I can't hold it in.

Nick's hands slide into his pocket, putting the bunch of keys out of reach from me, before taking his hand to my chin where he starts caressing my jawline with his thumb.

I know for a fact that Patricia is staring at me, I can feel her gaze burning holes in my back, but I don't move.

His thumb starts stroking my lips, and then he cups his whole hand around my chin and cheek.

"A kiss for a moment with your friend", he whispers and I do actually lean in closer, quickly pecking his lips and then sliding out of his grip.He did say I would get to meet her if I kissed her in his room, which I did, but I don't have time to argue about the other kiss right now because right now I have to talk to Patricia: calm her down.

I sit down beside her on the mattress and put my arms around her. At first, she's really tense, probably confused too since she saw me kiss my kidnapper, but then she welcomes my embrace and starts crying against my shoulder as I rub her back, whispering soothing words in her ear.

Nick is cold hearted enough to take out his phone and at first, I think he's typing something on the screen, but then I realize that he's taking a picture of Patricia and me.

I give him a mad glare, not wanting to say anything because of Patricia who is still leaning against my shoulder and who didn't see what Nick did.

I tell myself that I will ask him about the picture later and get him to delete it since I hate being with on photos, but something tells me I will forget to do it.

Minutes pass before Patricia calm down enough to breathe correctly but as she does, she gives me a forced smile as she pulls back from my embrace.

"Nick?" I call on him, my voice sounding extremely soft and light for a change. His head snaps up, he's been sitting with his phone for the last couple of minutes, and his dark eyes bore into mine.

"Can you leave us alone for a moment?" I ask, "please?"

He scoffs in response and then his facial expression becomes distant, as if he is considering it, but then my hopes are crushed as he slowly shakes his head.

"I don't kno-", he starts but I cut him off.

"Please?" His unsure countenance doesn't change, and I take a deep breath and slowly stands up, flashing Patricia a weak smile before turning my back to her and slowly walking towards Nick. He's sitting in the armchair and I bite my lip since I know he somehow finds it attractive, and slowly brush my fingertips against his arm, which is leaned on top of the armchair. I trace my fingers down from his upper arm to his own fingertips, and I can see his body tense up.

"Please?" I repeat once again, letting my fingers rest on top of his before moving them up to his face. I follow his chiseled jawline, knowing he's enjoying it. I can see the lust in his eyes.

I know I shouldn't be doing this, seducing him, and I wonder when I became this desperate. I think it was earlier today when I said his kisses didn't matter: when I lied.

Nick is just a guy with hormones, which I'm exploiting for my own winning, to get what I want. I hate every second I have to touch him,

I hate that this is how I have to act to get my will through, but I've always been extremely stubborn, and if this is what I have to do to get what I want, I'll do it. For me, it's just an act, like a school play you're forced to participate in.

I can hear Nick groan in frustration, unsure of what to do, and he grabs after me but I quickly take a step back, out of his reach. He groans again.

"Stop teasing me!"

"Then let us girl talk privately", I say, forcing a smug smirk onto my lips.

To my own frustration, he still doesn't give in to my wish, and I start playing with his hair and pout at him with my lips and give him my best puppy eyes.

"Fine!", he finally sighs, "you got ten minutes."

I immediately take a step back, away from him, and watch him get up. I expect him to walk straight to the door and therefore, I start walking back to Patricia, but Nick grabs a hold onto my hips and pulls me into his body.

"Don't think you get away that easily", he whispers huskily in my ear, "you can't just seduce me like that and then leave me hanging." He turns me around, so that I'm facing his chest due our height difference, and I turn my head away, feeling a blush forming on my cheeks.

"We got company", I mumble, feeling extremely uncomfortable since I know that Patricia is watching the show I'm putting up.

"I don't care about if she's watching or not", Nick smirks and takes a soft grip on my chin.

"But I do", I say and turn my face away again, causing Nick's hand to fall down his side from my chin.

He takes a few steps forward, making me walking backward, following his moves, and we stop in front of the door.

Nick reaches his hand into his pocket, picks up the bunch of keys and unlocking the door and stepping out with one arm around me, forcing me to him while whispering; "Then we'll do it outside."

I curse under my breath, not wanting to kiss him, give him another make-out session which I know he's expecting.

Nick doesn't even bother to lock the door as we stepped out, because instead, he slams the door shut by pushing me against it, not gentle nor harsh. I can't stop a small whimpering sound escape my throat and he smirks and 'tsk' at me.

"Oh, gorgeous", he sighs in amusement, "you're really interesting, you know that? Until yesterday, you would fight me every time I tried to kiss or even be near you, and look at you know. You're pretending like the kisses and closeness don't affect you, but your eyes give you away, and don't even think for a second that I bought the act you just performed. I know you still dislike the kisses, I know you don't like me, but you know what? I don't really care because I've made progress. Soon, you'll learn to like me."

I scoff at his words, figuring out that it doesn't matter if I talk back to him or not since I know for sure he's still gonna kiss me.

"Like you?" I say, raising my eyebrows at the same time, "you think I'll ever like you? Ha, that's gotta be the joke of the year. You're not my type, at all."

"I'm everyone's type", he smirks and I shake my head,my hair dancing around my face as I do so and I quickly flip all my hair over to one side and starts playing with it, an old habit I'm used to doing as I'm nervous. I don't like the fact that Nick could see through my act, even though I could see it coming, but most of all, I don't like the thought of what he'd said, that he'd made progress. That made me wonder, had he? What he had said is true, yesterday I could barely stand the kisses and now, here I am, kissing him like nothing. Or maybe not like nothing, but you get my point.

I furrow my eyebrows together in an attempt of pushing away my nervousness, and it worked.

I've always been good at hiding my feelings, but maybe it's because if these circumstances that it seems harder than usual?

"You know", I tell Nick, "you're wrong. You're really not my type, honestly. I don't like guys who are desperate enough to kidnap and mistreat the girl they want."

I thought Nick eyes would turn dark in anger at my words, but instead, they turn black with lust.

"I love how you put up a fight all the time", he murmurs, leaning in closer, "and I do love to see how you're slowly giving in. Before you know it, you've fallen head over heels for me."

Before I'm able to talk back, his lips attack my neck in wet, but still not sloppy, kisses. One of his hands finds it's way to my waist, as the other one pushes me gently against the wall, preventing me from moving away.

The kisses soon turn from gentle to harsh and as I feel him start to gentle bite on my soft skin, I twist my head in his direction, opening my lips slightly to beg him to stop, but just as I'm about to do so, he founds my soft spot and my whole body stiffens.

Shoot.

He smirks against my neck, noticing my reaction and understanding what he has found, and I try my hardest not to moan.

I place my hands on his chest and try to push him away, but it's like moving a wall, he doesn't move an inch.

A long list of curse words forms in my head, but I don't utter them out loud.

I move my hands from his chest to his face, cupping his chin and forcefully lifting it up, separating his lips from my skin, which he doesn't seem too happy with. He groans in frustration, but before he has the time to get back to his work, I crash my lips onto his, and it doesn't take him long to respond. I keep my eyes closed during the kiss, preventing the tears that have filled my eyes from falling. I don't let him into my mouth, which only frustrates him even more, but I do play with his hair during the long lasting kiss, and I feel his nails digging into my hips due to his firm grip.

Nick finally pulls away when we're both out of air, and he smirks at me, showing off his blinding white teeth.

"We gotta do this more often", he breathes out before letting go of me.

"Or never", I mumble, "I'm good with never."

And with those words left hanging, I turn towards the door to go back to Patricia, but I stop just as I'm about to close it, remember I forgot to ask him something important.

"Uhm, Nick?"

"Yes?" he looks at me with a sneer playing on his lips, like if he was expecting me to say something, which I think he actually did.

"How much time do I got? Oh, and, um... is there any cameras or something in there?" I wanted our talk to be as private as possible and knowing if he could hear us or something would be appreciated.

He moistens his lips and combs through his hair with his hand as he thinks about my question.

"I said ten minutes before, but I'll give you fifteen, no more, no less. And yes, there's a camera in the room."

I furrow my eyebrows in dismay.

"Can you hear what we're saying too?"

Nick chuckles darkly at that, and gently push me back a step so that my whole body is inside of the room.

"Now, that's something you'll have to figure out on your own", he smirks and closes the door right in my face.

I turn around, facing the room and Patricia, and my eyes immediately land on a small black camera in the far upper corner of the room. I sigh and meet Patricia's confused gaze. With Nick no longer present, she's acting far more like herself.

She looks at me with an unreadable expression and speaks up, much more confident now than a few minutes ago.

"What the hell is going on?"

Chapter 26: Weakness

I've realized that I failed miserably with making Patricia feel better, calmer. I've told her everything I know about what's going on with these kidnappings, and I've made it crystal clear about my feelings towards Nick. With other words; I've told her about how much I hate that disgusting, annoying, obnoxious, possessive maniac, and I said it out loud along with a list if curses, in case he could hear it through the door or camera.

Now, Patricia is whispering something in my ear, covering her lips with her hands - making sure no one can't hear or figure out what she's saying.

Her breath almost tickles against my ear, but her words make my eyes go wide and I stare at her with open mouth.

"You serious?" I whisper-yell, not caring about if someone hears, it's not like they know what we're talking about anyways.

But I know, and my heart feels lighter all of a sudden. She told me something that gave me hope, that lit a fire in my heart.

She told me Lindsey know about her being kidnapped and Peter being a part of the kidnapping in the school. Patricia just said that she's almost one hundred percent sure that Lindsey heard the short conversation she had with Nick right before she got kidnapped, that Lindsey heard it through her phone.

We both know for a fact that Lindsey never hangs up on a phone call if you've told her you'll be back in a few minutes.

I'm so happy right now, that I can't stop a smile from cracking onto my lips, and right then, a key twist in the door lock and Nick steps in.

"Time's up", he says, "you better say goodbye and..." His words died out as he got his eyes on me, and he then managed to breathe out one word, barely above a whisper; "wow..."

I give him a look full of confusion, and then I remember the smile on my face, the smile of pure happiness, and it quickly fades out.

He seems to finally get himself together and find his voice again, and his eyes show something I haven't seen before.

Could it be... love?

No, I push the thought away, it couldn't be.

"The smile of yours is breathtaking, gorgeous", he says with a smirk, fully recovered from the surprise, "you should wear it more often."

He almost succeeds with ruining my good mood completely, but I hang on to it like if it was my most precious belonging.

"Then give me a reason too", I say in a high pitched tone.

He takes the few steps that're laying between us, and Patricia instantly pulls back.

"I'm working on it", he says and caresses my cheek, "but now it's time to get out of here and get something to eat, and maybe tell me the reason for the sudden change of mood?"

I bite my lip, thinking, and then glance at Patricia.

"What about her? You just gonna leave her here?"

Nick shrugs and his face has gone to completely blank.

"Yeah, why not? Someone will come down and give her food later, she'll be fine."

I give him my best puppy eyes.

"But-"

"No buts", he cuts me off and takes a gentle but strong grip around my arm. Knowing I can't convince him, I give Patricia a quick hug and then follow Nick outside. As the door is about to close with her on the inside and me in the outside, I flash her a weak smile, which she returns.

Nick then move his hand from my arm to my waist and leads me to the kitchen.

Nick's POV

I look at Alex as she eats the last of the food I've warmed up to us. My own plate is empty, the food long gone, and all my focus lays on her.

I can't seem to get the picture of her smiling out of my head. With that smile on her face, she looked like a completely different person. She looked cute, not hot or sexy, but extremely beautiful and adorable, and it melted my heart.

But along with the picture, I can't stop thinking, wondering, what's the reason behind it. I've asked her, but all she did was saying she's happy to talk to a real friend again. I know she's lying, and I gonna figure out what.

If she won't tell me, Patricia will. It doesn't matter what I have to do to make her talk, if I want something, I get it.

But right now, I'm going to work on the thing I want most, Alex.

Like the bad boy I am, it's hard to admit it, but I think my liking for Alex has gone a step further.

Before, I liked her because she was hot and feisty, but now, I'm not only falling for her looks, but also for her personality.

It sure as hell is annoying, but I like her attitude.

It sure as hell driving me nuts, but I like how she never gives up, even though it might seem like it.

I love how she responds to my kisses, even though I know she's only doing it to get what she wants, but it's fine by me. I love her stubbornness, I think it's cute that she's trying her best even though I'm in control.

And most of all, I've fallen head over heels over her icing blue eyes and adorable smile.

Too bad for her that I'm not one of these guys who changes when they fall in love. I will remain as I am, and I will continue doing what I want, to get what I want.

And right now, I want her. Every part of her.

I want her heart, body, and trust.

And I won't give up, but continue trying until I succeed.

Alex's POV

I put my fork down, my plate now empty. Nick has stared at me for minutes now, and his gaze is really disturbing, but I try my best to ignore it.

I look around the kitchen, my own eyes flickering over the table to the sink, and then on Nick.

He smirks at me and stands up, putting both of our dishes in the sink and turning to face me.

"Let's go and change, we gonna work out again", he tells me, and I know by the look on his face that's not worth arguing about.

I follow him down to his room and quickly take the clothes he gives me and lock myself in the bathroom, and groan in frustration. It's the same clothes that I was given the last time I was going to train and I reluctantly strip out if my clothes and put on the new ones. I hate the length of the short and the fact that I was only given a sports bra as a top, and I do exactly as last time. I put on my old shirt over the bra and examine myself in the mirror.

I thought I would look somewhat different, less living and with dull and puffy eyes, but I don't. I look normal, like always. My icing blue eyes that seem to see straight into your soul are as captivating as before, and my plump lips do still have the same strawberry red shade. It's fascinating how something can seem to be so normal on the outside when it's the straight opposite.

With a sigh, I put my hair into a messy ponytail, not caring about how it looks, and I suddenly freezes. On my neck, fully visible to anyone, is a hickey.

He's given me a freaking hickey.

I quickly put on some makeup to hide it, not wanting to give him the satisfaction of seeing it, and then I step out from the bathroom.

Nick's head immediately snap towards me and I realized, both shocked and horrified, that I just walked in on him changing.

I stare at him for a couple of seconds, startled, until he speaks up and I snap out of it.

"You know, you don't have to watch it from afar. You're even allowed to touch it", he smirks and I feel a blush heat up my cheeks.

"Sorry, I just gonna-"

"Stay", he cuts me off and I shake my head and start to back into the bathroom but he quickly throws the shirt in his hand onto the bed and walks up to me. I try to slam the door shut in his face, but he puts his hand on it and forced it wide open and drags me out.

He traps me between the wall and his body, again, but this time I'm not in the mood to play, and I dive under his arm to get away. I don't come far before his arms slip around my waist and my back is slammed into his chest.

"It's not nice to run away like that", he mumbles into the crook of my neck before gently pecking it.

"It feels like a setback, you know?" He says, "it went so good earlier today."

I sigh and stop fighting against his grip.

"Nothing is going well around here", I say harshly, "the fact that I have to kiss you is a proof of how everything's gone to hell."

He chuckles darkly, his chest vibrating.

"You said yourself that you didn't care about it."

It feels like I'm going to explode any second. I didn't know everything I kept inside of me, all emotions I'm trying to hide, would come up to the surface at the same time.

"I lied, okay?!" I squeal and start fighting against his grip again.

"Sch..." He hushes and turns me around, do that my face is facing his chest.

"Calm down..." He caresses my cheek and then brings me into a tight hug. I don't hug back and I don't move back. I just stand still until he finally pulls away.

I've managed to push away all of the emotions that were laying on the surface but I wish that I would be able to push Nick away too.

"Gorgeous..."

"Leave me alone."

That was probably the wrong thing to say because Nick suddenly takes a leap towards me and a surprised shriek escapes my throat as I feel my body launch backward together with his. And then we land onto something soft that sinks down under our weight. The bed.

"What the fudge?" I groan and tries to get up, but Nick is faster and manages to straddle himself over my waist.

He takes my hands in one of his and keeps them pinned down, and then he starts tickling me with his free hand.

He. Is. So. Dead.

A bubbling laugh escapes my lips as I squirm under his touch, and a smile cracks onto his lips.

"I-I... h-hate... y... ou..." I managed to breath out between my laughs, and he chuckles.

"Love you too", he says and finally removes his damn fingertips from my stomach, only to quickly lean in and kiss me on my lips.

He still holds my hands in s death grip, and he pushed me down with his own body weight. I can't do anything, and he quickly moves down to my neck.

"You shouldn't hide the beautiful mark I gave you", he says and wipes the makeup off, exposing the hickey he made.

"Much better", he smirks, "but there's still one thing left. Your shirt. I don't recall telling you that you could wear it."

"You didn't tell me not to wear it either", I reply and he gives me a glare.

"Don't try to be smart with me", he spits, "either you take it off, or I take it off for you."

He releases my hands, but all I do is placing them on his chest in an attempt to push him off of me, but I fail and am just about to take my hands off of his chest when he placed his own on top of mine.

"You can't say that you don't like what you see", he says and I shake my head.

"You got abs, so what? It's not like I'm going to start liking you because of the fact that you got a hot body."

His lips turn into a smirk and he gives me a wink.

"You think my body is hot?"

I mentally faceplant myself. Okay, I admit that he got a good looking body with abs and a six pack, but so what? That doesn't change anything.

"Aren't we supposed to train or something?" I ask, changing the subject.

"Well, yeah we are, as soon as you taken off... this." He grips the hem of my shirt and I open my mouth slightly, but no words come out and I just shake my head.

He flashes me a crooked smile and starts tugging at the hem, exposing my flat stomach.

I find my words again as I start squirming under him.

"No!"

"Oh, yes", he chuckles and pull the shirt upwards towards my face.

"Please don't..." I plead, for nothing.

All I got is a kiss from Nick because he suddenly stops with undressing me off my shirt and kisses me on my lips instead.

The kiss doesn't last long, but still long enough for me to lose patient and bite his bottom lip to get rid of him.

He pulls back, smirking.

"Feisty now, aren't we?"

"Just stop! I do it myself, okay?" I shout, not able to take his slow torture anymore. He releases my hands from his grip and gestures for me to start.

"Go on then, we don't have all day."

I glare at him.

"Would you mind getting off of me?" I spit.

"Yes, I would", he answers and I groan, knowing that getting him off of me is as easy as pushing away a wall, with other words, nearly impossible.

Slowly and with slightly shaking hands, I grip the hem of my shirt. I know it may not seem like a big deal to only wear a sports bra as a top, a lot of people do it, but with Nick forcing me to, it feels completely different.

I take a deep breath and get it over with as fast as possible. I pull it over my head, messing up my hair even further, and throw the shirt on the floor.

"Happy now?"

Nick moistens his lips and looks at me, but not on my face, though.

Ugh.

"You, gorgeous, got an amazing body."

I sigh.

"Yeah, everything with me is amazing. My eyes, my body, my personality and blah blah blah", I say with every single word dripping of sarcasm.

Nick starts trailing his fingertips down my side, causing shivers to send down my spine, and with his free hand he gently strokes some hair away from my face.

"You are amazing", he says and then, once again, kisses me.

I don't know why, but the fact that he said I was amazing, instead of something like hot or sexy, made my heart feel warmer for a short, short second - before I remembered who it was that said it.

"This will all be over sooner if you kiss back", he says, but I don't.

I can feel his body heat radiating off on me and he presses his tense body against mine. If he wouldn't be a psychopath, if he wouldn't have kidnapped me, this would all be completely different. I might've actually liked him then, but too bad his whole personality ruins it.

When he finally pulls back, he also gets off of me and I quickly get out of the bed.

"Why do you always seem to be in such a hurry?" he asks as his arms slip around my uncovered waist and lead me towards the door.

"Because I always have something to run away from", I answer as we walk through it.

His only response to that is a dark chuckle and I throw a wistful glance at the door to where Patricia is kept as we pass it.

I thought that we would go back to the room I was in last time I trained, but no, when Nick opens up the door leading into where we are going to be the coming hours, my jaw drops.

I honestly have no idea of how big this house is, but I've just stepped into a freaking climbing room, with several meters high climbing walls.

"Seriously?" I breath out, "climbing? When will I ever need to climb like that?" I ask, nodding at a person who's currently taking on the hardest wall. I think it's Vince, but I'm not sure.

"You never know when it might come in handy", Nick whispers in my ear and pushes me further into the room.

Even though the room isn't that big, I'm still surprised that they have it. I mean, who got a full set of climbing walls in their own house?

Clearly they do, but still.

This room must reach up to the floor above, at least, but I wouldn't be surprised if this is three floors high in total.

"Put this on", Nick tells me and hands me a sit harness.

I put it on, not in the mood to fight since I know I will lose, and as I'm done I realize Nick has put on one too, and my lips curl upwards at the sight.

"Kirk will secure you", Nick tells me, "and Zeke secures me. I hope you know how to climb and if you don't, I'll teach you."

I sigh, still not understanding the point of this.

"Just tell me why I need to know how to do this? Your answer about how it might come in handy is too vague."

"Let's just say that we don't only kidnap girls to get money. And with all the other things we do, climbing might come in handy."

We walk to Kirk and Zeke who secures us, but I keep the conversation going.

"And your point is what?"

Nick shakes his head with a smirk playing on his lips.

"You don't get it, do you?" he says, "you're not going back home, ever. You're gonna stay here with us, you're going to be a part of us."

I almost choke at his words.

"A part of you?" I shriek, ignoring the surprised stares from everyone else in the room, "I will never be a part of you guys. I will get home and I will get you guys arrested."

Nick smiles at me as he leads me to one of the easier climbing walls.

"It's cute how you still have fate, but you should just shut your gorgeous mouth and start climbing."

And so I did.

* * *

I don't know how long time we climb but every muscle in my body is aching when we're finally done.

"I admit", Nick says with a heavy breathing, " that you're pretty good for being untrained."

Ignoring what Nick just said, I take off the sit harness. I did make it pretty far on the harder walls, but I didn't succeed climbing all the way up on any of them when I had to follow a certain track, like only gripping the red grips.

Now, my hands are sore and full of blisters.

Everyone from the climbing room heads into the kitchen, where someone already ordered pizza for us to take, and we all start to eat.

I'm not really having that much of an appetite, and only take one slice which I'm slowly chewing on as everyone else of the guys seems to throw themselves over the pieces.

On the opposite side of the room, I catch a glimpse of the other girls but as stand up from my place on one of the sofas to go to them, Nick holds me back.

"Hey!" someone shouts and I snap my head into the direction of the voice and recognize it as Will, "you guys gotta make some space for me too, don't think I will stand when I know that I can get a place to sit."

"Sorry, but it's full", Zeke replies with amusement in his voice and Will turn his face towards Nick instead.

"You", he says, "get your girlfriend to sit in your lap or something."

"I'm not his girlf-" I start to protest but Nick cuts me off by sneaking his arm around my waist and practically lifting me into his lap.

"Oh, yes you are", he smiles and everyone in the room laughs at my reaction, except for the other girls.

I notice that Peter's not here, but I don't dare to ask why.

These guys do scare me, even though it might not seem like it at all times, and now when they are all gathered together my fear only increases.

After all, this is the guys that ruined my life.

I hate them, and I hate how they can seem to take all of this so damn normal.

I hope, with my whole heart, they Lindsey will find a way to get us out of here.

Nick put his hand on my thigh, and I quickly slap it away, only to find him doing it again moments later. He seems to be amused by my reaction and continue to do so and right as I'm about to explode, telling him to stop along with a long list of curses, Zeke speaks up.

"We're going to the black market next week", he says and immediately catches my attention even though his talking to the other guys, and not me.

"Aubrey has been here almost a month now, and we still haven't gotten any money for her. You guys already knew that we would go there, but now it's settled that we do it on Wednesday. The other girls do still have some time left before we need the ransom money, but it seems like Nick already made up his mind about Alex."

My body tense up as everyone's eyes dart towards me and Nick, and I can feel him tighten the grip around my waist.

"You gonna keep her?" Zeke asks as if I'm some stupid toy or puppy.

Nick nods, "yes, I'm gonna keep her."

His words send chillers down my spine.

I know that he'd said it many times before but now, with everyone listening, it almost feels like he confirms it.

"Lighten up, buttercup", I hear Kirk say, "you should be glad that you're not getting into the black market as Aubrey."

As he mentions Aubrey, she whimpers loudly and starts to cry. I understand her. They are talking about selling her to who knows.

"You're terrible, all of you", I say slowly, not believing myself to have the guts to.

"What did you say?" Zeke asks and I gulp, trying to gain as much confidence as possible. I can feel Nick tense up underneath me, but I don't care.

"You are talking about her life like if it's nothing", I say. "You are going to sell her for freaking sake! Can't you see how wrong and completely sick that is? Don't you have a heart at all? Look at her! She's just a girl, she has her whole life in front of her but you're ruining it. You are a monster, you all are."

"Alex..." Nick says in a warning tone but I keep my head held high and stare at Zeke. I don't like him the slightest anymore. Not after what he just said.

"If you think it's so wrong, then why don't you take her place?" he suggests and before I have time to say anything, Nick speaks for me.

"No! She's not going to do anything. Alex, if you don't shut up right now, I swear I will make you."

Zeke arch an eyebrow at me. "You better listen to your boyfriend before you get into serious trouble. You know, Alex, I've seen from the start that you got an attitude, but you really gotta watch it before you take it too far."

"Or what?", I say with a challenging tone, "you gonna hurt me or sell me? Go ahead, it's not like it's gonna be worse than-"

"That's it!" Nick snaps, quickly standing up and almost causing me to fall down to the ground if it wasn't for the hard grip he'd taken on my arm.

"What has gotten into you?" he shouts angrily as he drags me out of the room and down the stairs, "you're practically begging for death."

"What has gotten into me?" I shout back, "is that I'm tired of being stuck here. Don't you see? This, being here, isn't living. It's surviving. I can't do or say what I want and I'm being treated like a damn dog! Not being able to be myself is driving me crazy."

"But still you're having it much better than many others", Nick says through gritted teeth and opens up the door into his bedroom.

"And what's that supposed to mean?" I snap and rip myself arm out of his grip.

"That means", he shuts the door loudly and locks it, "that you're having it a thousand times better than many others. I don't hit you, instead, I protect you from those who want to. I don't rape you like many other guys do to their girls, and I give you food and a nice place to sleep. But you're too damn stubborn to see that. All you see when you look at me is a monster, but I'm the one who's currently keeping you safe. If there would be any other that would've chosen you, like Will or Kirk, you would've been beaten blue and bloody by now if you kept that attitude of yours."

"So what you mean is that you're not the devil, but my guardian angel?" My voice is dripping with venom and I'm glaring daggers at him.

"What I'm saying", Nick sighs, "is that you should rethink your situation and be grateful."

I give out a dry laugh. "Grateful? For what? Being kidnapped? For being ripped apart from my life? Yeah, you're right, I should be grateful. So thank you so so so damn much. You have no idea of how glad I am that Patricia fou-". I choke on the last word, realizing what I'm about to say. My eyes widen and I press my lips tightly together and mentally curse myself over and over again.

Shit.

I lost control of my thoughts, I snapped and almost gave out my only hope of getting out of here, and now I've caught Nick's fully attention.

"Glad that Patricia what?" Nick asks, slightly amused at my shocked facial expression but at the same time extremely determined to find out what I'm hiding.

"Nothing", I say way too quickly for acting normal.

"Alex..." he warns, "I know you're hiding something and I want to know what."

I look him dead in the eye.

"But we don't always get as we want, do we?" I can see him clench his fist together at my words.

"Alex, seriously. Lay off with that attitude. I know I said I don't hit you but you are seriously getting on my nerves right now."

My anger has gone far too long for be to being able to control it and I spit, actually spit, Nick in the face.

"Screw you."

The next thing I know is a stinging sensation in my cheek.

I slowly lift my fingertips to the sore spot and then look at Nick with hatred. His one hand is lifted, the other one still clenched.

"Fine", he says with absolute no emotions at all, "if you won't tell me Patricia will. And I won't hesitate to hurt her if I need to. Or maybe I'll do it anyway, to teach you a lesson. Ever heard of the term 'whipping boy'? A person who take the punishment for someone else, a scapegoat? Maybe Patricia should be yours. "

I stare at him in disbelief.

"No! You can't... you wouldn't..."

He flashes me a sinister sneer and starts to walk towards me.

"Oh yes, I can and I will."

For every step he takes forward, I take as many backward but I soon hit the wall and he gives out a dark chuckle.

"Not so feisty anymore, are we?" He places his head on either side of my head, trapping me, and I look down at my feet.

"Look at me", he whispers in my ear and starts nibbling on my earlobe for a few seconds before pulling back, allowing me to raise my head up - which I don't.

"The more you defy me, the more pain I'll inflict on Patricia."

My head snaps up and my piercing blue eyes meets his cold and dark ones.

"Good girl", he whispers, "now kiss me. The better you do it, the better it will be for Patricia."

I hate him. I hate him with every bone in my body, for every beat my heart takes, hate flows through my veins.

"Why are you doing this?" I whisper, not being able to hold back a few tears from filling my eyes. He takes my chin in his hands and caresses my cheek, wiping away the few tears that fall down.

"Because I like you. I like you so damn much and I don't want you to escape. And I want to win the bet. I told you I would break you, and I think I just figured out how."

I think so too.

More tears fill my eyes as I lean into the few centimeters that lay between our lips. Right as I'm about to kiss him, I take a shaky breath and breath in his cologne.

"Please don't hurt her", I plead, my lips brushing against his. Before he has time to answer, I press my lips, salty because of my tears, against his completely.

For the first time in what feels like forever, I imagine myself kissing someone else instead of Nick.

I imagine myself kissing Shane, my latest ex, because even though I despise him, he's a thousand times better than Nick.

When the kiss is over, Nick pulls away with a smile and leaves the room, heading to Patricia with the sound of my heart breaking screams filling the air.

I bang at the door until my hands are sore and bloody, and I scream at the top of my lungs for him to not hurt her until my throat is too sore for me to utter a single word, and I cry until I no longer have any tears left.

My screams become mixed with Patricia's for a while, before I slide down the wall completely dried out of energy.

Her screams do luckily not last long and I figure she's told him our secret, my hope.

Congrats, Nick. You're going to win. You found a way to break me.

Unless Lindsey and the police work really fast, it's time for be to say goodbye life and hello hell.

But it's not game over quite yet.

I'm going to fight until the end.

Chapter 27: Waiting

Lindsey's POV

I sit on a white couch in my living room with a cup of hot tea in my hands. My mom pops into the room every ten minutes to check on me, but I wave her off, telling her I want to be alone.

My phone is laying on the small table in front of me and I'm waiting for it to ring, even though I know it can take days before I get the call I'm waiting on.

After the confusing yet terrifying call I had with Patricia the other night, I can't seem to concentrate on anything at all.

First, my best friend got kidnapped and now, my other close friend has met the same faith. I heard everything she said with that guy and as it ended and no one replied to my screams through the phone,

I immediately called the police and had an officer over within ten minutes.

They managed to get access to the whole call, from the start to the end, but that Nick guy that took my friends was smart, he didn't give out any specific information. But, the officer said that they found one thing of interest, except for the fact that they got a strong reason to arrest Peter, and that is what Nick said about the black market.

Peter.

I hate him.

I hate him so freaking much.

How dare he betray us? His friends.

Currently, he's down at the station, where he's been kept since the police managed to get their hands on him.

They say that they don't have proof enough to actually judge him for the crimes I'm almost sure he's committed.

Yes, I don't know it for a fact, I haven't seen it with my own eyes, but I do trust Patricia and everything I heard on the phone.

Now, I'm waiting for the police to call and inform me about how the investigation's going.

I really don't care about what they are doing, all I care about is getting my friends back.

Since I'm the one who brought the information in, and since I'm one of the closest people to some of the people that's kidnapped, the centre of this life-changing problem, the police told me that they are trying to find out where the black market will take place because if they find the kidnappers, they will also find the kidnapped one way or another.

I'm relying on the police, but it's not like I have any other choice. I can't find them on my own.

"Sweetie, are you sure you don't want anything?" My mom asks, coming into the living room once again and causing me to snap back to reality.

"Uhm, no. I'm fine", I say in a distant tone. It's all I've been lately. Distant.

My other friends at school are worried about me, my family is worried about me, and I, I am worried about Alex and Patricia.

With a sigh I sink deeper into the cushions, my eyes never leaving my phone.

Alex's POV

Nick never came back last night. I somehow managed to fall asleep leaned against the wall by the door, completely empty and drawn out on energy.

The clock shows that it's now 10:16 AM but I don't bother getting up. I mean, what's the point?

I can't get out of here and I still feel exhausted. My throat's still dry, my knuckles still bloody, but it doesn't matter right now.

I don't have to talk to anyone and I don't have to use my hands. I don't have to do anything and therefore, I will just stay here in the corner, hoping that I will slowly fade out, vanish.

Of course, that doesn't happen.

As the clock switch from 10:39 to 10:40 AM, I hear the sound of footsteps outside the door and the sound of a key turning in a lock.

The door slowly opens, the sudden light stinging in my eyes, but I remain on my place on the floor.

"Alex?" I hear Nick ask with surprise in his voice.

I don't answer him and he continues.

"Alex? What the hell are you doing? Alex, are you alright?"

He kneels down in front of me, his fingers stroking gently over my pale cheek. My body stiffens at his touch and I can hear him sigh.

"C'mon gorgeous, I won't hurt you."

But you did last night.

He slowly stands up, closing and locking the door, before he crouches down on the same spot as before.

"Go ahead", he says in a voice barely above a whisper, and I furrow my eyebrow slightly but I still ignore him.

"Go ahead and tell me how much you hate me, scream it out for everyone to hear if that's what it takes to make you feel better. You can even hit me if you want, it's not more than fair."

Fair? Hitting him once wouldn't make it fair between us. He ruined my life and kidnapped me, and hurt my friend. And he thinks that one punch will make it alright?

I continue to ignore him but I can feel the anger bubbling up to the surface again.

Yes, I do want to hit him, but that would mean that I listen to him, which I won't.

I've already told him, more than once, how much I hate him and punch him now when he let me, it's not the same thing.

It's no point in doing it when you're allowed to.

"Oh shit", Nick suddenly burst out, "your knuckles, Alex."

The pain caused by my sore knuckles is nothing compared to the pain he caused me emotionally.

"If you don't stand up now and listen to me", he warns, "I swear I will pick you up myself."

I still don't move, and I then feel his arms sneak around me, picking me up bridal style. I hate that he's touching me, but I don't want him to see that I care. I'm just going to be silent and not show any emotions at all.

He places me on the counter in his bathroom and picks up a first aid kit from one of the drawers.

"This might sting a little", he says as he holds a cotton ball in his hand with cleaning alcohol on it, which he starts dab on my sore knuckles.

I flinch at the sudden stinging pain, my only show of emotion, but Nick holds my hand in a strong grip, keeping it in place and continue taking care of my wounds.

I bite myself on my bottom lip to not give away any sound and when he's done, my knuckles are clean and swathed.

Even though Nick's done, he doesn't release his grip on my hand, and he clears his throat before speaking.

"I'm not gonna say I'm sorry for hurting Patricia, because I'm not. And I do know what you were hiding from me, and it has caused us trouble, but I am truly sorry for hurting you."

Like if I care.

"Alex, please talk to me. Every time it feels like we've made progress, something happens that take us back to how it was at first. You hating me and refusing to do as I say. The other guys are getting tired of you. All you do is causing us trouble. But I won't give up on you. You can't fight forever Alex, and I will be here when you finally give up.

I'll always be here, Alex. It doesn't matter if you hate me and don't want me to be because I won't leave, and neither will you."

Chapter 28: Freedom

What has happened to my life, and most importantly, what have I done to deserve it?

I've never been a goody two-shoes but neither have I been a trouble-maker and look where it have gotten me.

I'm stuck in a hellhole worse than school and if that isn't bad, I don't know what is.

I hate it here, because here, I'm cut off from the most important thing in my whole life.

Freedom.

Life without it doesn't even deserve to be called living, it's surviving. I need my freedom, I need to be able to be who I want to be and do what I want to do. If you always do as other people tells you to, they are going to expect more and more of you until you reach the limit where you are no longer yourself, but a shell formed by the people around you.

I can't stand being told what to do all the time and thrown from one to another like some kind of a ball or toy.

I'm a human, with a heart and feeling, but something tells me that everyone haven't gotten it into their small brains yet.

I'm wearing invisible chains which I have to get out of, and that fast.

I've had one breakdown and I can't risk another one. I don't know how strong I am. I don't know how much I can take before I finally break down completely - until I lose the bet I'm desperately trying to win.

To be honest, I don't even know what I'm doing here.

Sure, Nick says he likes me but we all know how well that's going, and all I'm doing on the days is either nothing or something pointless as climbing or watching the guys play video games.

I don't belong here. I never have and I never will, but Nick is too damn selfish to let me go and I'm too entangled in this mess to get out with ease.

If I get out, I can almost swear on that Nick will hurt Patricia, which means that I have to take her with me, but in order to do that, I need to find a way out first.

But I can't just ditch the other girls, and therefore, I have to go to the police the first thing I do if I ever get out of here, but the police station is also one of the first places where they will look, but honestly, I think they would look anywhere and nowhere in order to find me if I managed to escape. At least Nick would, I think.

I can always hope that it isn't right, that I'm just a silly girl in his eyes, but something tells me that I'm not that lucky.

Ugh, I know it's a terrible sign when someone, in this case Nick, makes Shane, my ex, look like an angel in comparison.

I don't like to think about my past, I prefer standing strong and moving.

The past is in the past, you can't change what has happened or what you've done, but you can change yourself.

Sometimes, you even change without knowing or wanting it.

Like now.

I'm not the same person as before.

I don't act like I did a few days ago before my life turned upside down.

I don't say what I would've said a few days ago.

I don't even think as I would have a few days ago, because if I would, I wouldn't be thinking about Shane right now.

I wouldn't be thinking this much at all, but now it seems like it's the only thing that I'm allowed to do, or at least I won't get caught because of it.

My mind is the only thing that Nick can't control, but truth to be told, not even I can control it at all times.

Currently, my mind is my getaway, a place where I do have freedom and a place where I can hide from reality for a moment, try to forget about everything.

Some people say that they escape reality for a moment by dive into their thoughts or listen to music, but I don't.

I can't escape reality, it will always be there no matter how much I try to get away from it, but I can hide from it, and hiding is exactly what I'm doing.

That is just another proof of how I've changed.

Before, I did say that I escaped reality as I showered and washed away all my worries for a moment but being here has learned me that it's impossible to do so.

Every time I dived into the shower, I didn't escape reality, I hid from it.

I found some comfort in the warmth and shielding it gave from reality.

Now, I find some comfort in zooming out of what' real, even though it might mean thinking about my past.

Nick left me in his room again hours ago as I totally refused to eat and he hasn't been back since. It's been hours now, hours where I've tried to think lovely thoughts, but my mind is now empty of happy memories, because I only got a limited amount if it, and now I got the bad left to think through.

I actually find it quite amusing how I think about Shane now with though about that my last words to him were 'I don't ever want to see or hear from you again'.

Harsh words? Yeah, I know, but trust me, he deserved it.

I guess that if you think it all through, the last years of my life, you'll realize that if it wasn't for Shane, I wouldn't be here now.

If it wasn't for Shane, I wouldn't be in this stupid town and I wouldn't be kidnapped by those stupid psychopath maniacs.

But, if it wouldn't be for Shane, I wouldn't have met my best friend Lindsey, or Patricia and all my other friend for that matter and that's the reason to why I would prefer to be with him over Nick.

Yes, Shane did mess up my life, he made a big mistake and he wasn't the only one who had to suffer the consequences for it, but he wasn't far as bad as Nick.

Shane was actually really sweet at first, the perfect boyfriend, but then everything kinda derailed and everything changed.

He changed, and not for the better.

I still really can't believe that he-

"Boo!"

I jump at the sudden sound coming from close to my ear and hear a dark, sadly familiar, chuckle behind me.

Nick.

"Whatcha doing?" he asks casually, "because it gotta be something really interesting for you to not hear me get in."

I can feel my cheeks turn a light shade of red and I feel stupid for not hearing him. I mean, how could I miss it?

I guess I really did snap out of reality for a while.

"Still giving me the silent treatment, huh?" Nick cocks an eyebrow at me but I don't meet his gaze, a clear answer to his question.

He sighs loudly.

"Patricia is okay, thought you would want to know that, and you are coming with my upstairs to eat. You really do not have any idea of how angry some of the guys are at you right now, Peter's busted because if you and I suggest you do as I tell you if you don't have a death wish."

My head snaps up as he mention Peter's name and I meet his dark eyes with a questioning look on my face, still not wanting to talk.

"Remember the secret Patricia told you? Well, it's all thanks to you that your other little friend tattled to the police."

A small smile crack onto my lips, I can't hold it back.

Lindsey told the police before someone had time to hush her, which I thought someone would as Nick figured out Patricia's and I's secret, but Lindsey made it to the police before someone made it to her.

Nick takes a rough hold onto my arm as he sees my smile, and he shakes me harshly.

"It's nothing to be glad for. You made everyone angry, you've caused us big trouble, and you're only making it worse for yourself."

I bite myself on my bottom lip as the smile slowly vanishes from my face.

"Good", Nick mutters as he sees my now sad countenance, "now let's go upstairs and eat, it's already late afternoon because we had to take care of the problem you caused "

It feels like a stone drop in my stomach at his words, and my heart speed increases almost immediately.

"What do you mean with 'take care of the problem'?" I ask, breaking my silent treatment.

I can feel my fingertips tingling and my breathing becoming uneven. The panic rising inside of me, bubbling up to the surface as I wait for an answer.

"That", Nick says, "is left for you to find out."

Chapter 29: Picture

Nick's POV

I don't get how people can be so nice, never hurting anyone, ever.

That's the easiest way to get things done. Hurt them or threaten to hurt them, it works almost all of the times, but it gets tricky when you don't want to hurt the person, and your threats don't work.

Like with Alex.

Then, you have to find their weakness. In this case, something as cliché as her friends.

Hurt them or threaten to, and you got yourself an angry but controllable Alex at your service.

I didn't want to make everything as bad as it is, but she left me with no choice.

Yes, I like Alex.

Yes, I know she hates me.

Yes, I know I messed everything up even more by hurting her friends.

No, I'm not sorry for doing it.

She needs to be taught a lesson or two but right now, she has to eat.

We're in the kitchen and she sits on one of the chairs by the island but she hasn't touched or even glanced at the plate with fried fries and chicken that's in front of her.

I bet it's cold by now too.

I sigh and look at her, pulling my hand restlessly through my hair.

Her raven hair falls down her shoulders in a mess but it still frames her face and brings out the icing blue in her eyes.

Even though she isn't even trying, she looks gorgeous.

I do feel lucky for having her, but I wish it was under different circumstances.

Truth to be told, I'm not a good guy. I never was and never will.

I want Alex more than I want anything else.

No, I'm not obsessed, even though that's the term she would use, but I enjoy her company at the same time as it's driving me nuts.

I admire her courage at the same time as I curse it.

I like her stubbornness at the same time as it annoys me.

I love her smile at the same time as I'm the one who washes it away.

I crave for her at the same time as I keep feeding her reasons to hate me.

And all of that am I doing because I want to keep her.

"You have to eat", I tell her but she doesn't respond. She's giving me the silent treatment and trust me when I say that I hate it.

She's acting like if I don't even exist. I sigh and decide to prove her that I sure as hell do.

I walk up to her and place myself close, very close, to her. Even though she's trying to hide it, I can feel her body tense up as my breathing hits her neck.

"Eat up", I command and as I still get no response, I wrap my arms securely around her waist, being able to do so thanks to the bar stool she's sitting on.

I wait for her reaction, but none come and I groan in frustration and start to slowly move my hands down to her thigh.

I'm almost starting to think that she, against all odds, won't say anything now either, but then I suddenly hear her bright voice, barely above a whisper.

"Please stop", she says and I obey. All I wanted from her was a reaction, which I got.

I move my hands back to her waist and then leave one there and trail up to her face with my other, stroking back a piece of hair behind her ear.

"If you don't pick up that fork right now, I gonna feed you, because you won't leave this room before the plate is empty", I say, trying to not sound too harsh.

I don't think she trusts me by my words because she keeps ignoring me and I pick up the fork with one hand and stab some fries on it, aiming at her mouth.

Halfway there, she grabs the fork from me, our fingers connection for a second before I let go, and she starts to slowly eat the food - reluctantly.

I stay by her side for a few minutes before sitting down beside her, and when she's finally done, after what feels like an eternity, I put her plate in the sink and take her hand in mine.

She tries to grab it from me, but I hold it in a firm grip and drags her towards the living room.

I sit down in one of the sofas, pulling her down with me, and holds her there as she attempts to get up. She attempts to get away, probably hating the fact that her body is laying on top of mine.

"What did you do to her?" she asks as she stops fighting and relaxes slightly in my arms, without any doubts talking about Lindsey.

"She's alive", I say vaguely, not wanting to give her any details.

"That's not the answer."

I look down at her. She's biting herself on her bottom lip, not on purpose, and it feels like she's missing something, a spark in her eyes.

I guess that I should be glad that she's not fighting against my any-more, not as much at least, but somehow I miss it.

I like when she's being feisty, that's a part of who she is.

"That's the answer you'll get", I tell her and rest my chin on the top of her head.

"I hate you", she says, but still she's staying in my arms.

Alex's POV:

He's touching me. He placed me in his lap for freaking sake. I hate it, and I hate him. Simple as that. The only reason to why I don't move, or even try to, is because I know that I will fail so what's the point?

Besides, I really want to know what they did to Lindsey, or not really want to, more like have to. The worry is slowly eating me up and all the strong feelings I feel are overwhelming.

Nick chuckle coldly as I tell him what I feel about him.

"You're cute when you're mad", he says, "and especially when you're biting your lip like that but you already knew that so I take it as a good sign that you still continue with it."

Dammit. I immediately stop biting and curse myself for it.

There's another thing that makes me frustrated.

He doesn't get angry.

I tell him that I hate him and he tells me I'm cute instead of telling me that I'm wrong or something. It's like he finds me being angry amusing, which he probably does.

I stretch out my arm to grab the remote to the tv and turn it on, surprisingly enough without getting stopped by Nick.

I flip through the channels until I found what I'm searching for.

The news.

"Alex..." Nick says in almost a pleading voice, "I'm not sure you should-"

"I'm fine", I cut him off and focus on the woman on the screen.

Her voice blast out from the speakers and I realize the newscast just began, and for a second I forget about Nick's hand that caress my hair and focus on the newswoman instead.

"The search for the still missing teenagers from Beckwith High School continues. By now the police have brought one student from the school whose name they won't give out, for questioning and the police are said to have a lead onto the kidnapper. What it is, on the other hand, is still unknown.

The newly reported missing student, Patricia Greendale, have yet not been heard of but it is strongly believed that she's been taken by the same kidnappers as the ones who attacked Beckwith High School.

It seems like the students can't have any more bad luck, but the most unlikely have sadly happened.

A close friend to the now two kidnapped girls, Alexandra Terres and Patricia Greendale, was attacked in her home last night. Lindsey McGordon, the victim for the serious assault that took place in her home only hours ago, is now treated at the hospital for major injuries. "

My breathing pick up a faster pace as I hear my best friends name and my eyes widen in horror at the words the newswoman is saying.

"Despite her bad state, she managed to tell an ambulance officer that the responsible for the assault were the Beckwith kidnappers. How she know is still a mystery for us outside the investigation but luckily the doctors said that she will be recovered. The reason behind the assault is still unknown."

As she finishes the sentence, the tv turns black and I realize Nick's taken the remote and pressed the off button.

"That's enough", Nick says with a stern voice and I jump up from my place before he has time to react and stop me.

I can feel tears filling my eyes, causing my sight to become blurry, and I stumble forward.

"That's enough?" I ask Nick, anger clearly audible in my voice, "but abusing Lindsey isn't?"

He slowly gets up and starts walking towards me, for every step he takes forward, I take one back.

"You brought it upon yourself this time", he says as I back into a wall, "you refused to tell us the secret you had with Patricia."

I slide, leaned against the wall, towards the direction of the kitchen.

"Like if you would have done differently if I told you", I spit.

Nick shrugs. "Maybe, maybe not. I guess it's all Patricia's fault, isn't it? She's the one who couldn't keep her mouth shut in the first place."

"You're the one who couldn't keep your dirty hands away from us in the first place", I counter and slip through the opening to the kitchen.

"You know what?" he says, following me inside, "let's make a new deal because neither you nor I can afford with your bullshit anymore. If you behave from now on, we'll release Patricia and leave Lindsey alone."

I shake my head, my hair dancing around my face.

"No. It's too late. I don't trust you at all. I won't make deals with the devil."

"Good that I'm not the devil then", Nick chuckles and eyes me intensely.

We're circling around the isle and it feels like I'm the victim and Nick the predator.

"Can you two just skip the drama already?" someone suddenly blurts out, causing me to jump out of my skin. Not literally.

Both Nick and I snap our head in the direction of the voice and there, leaned against the doorframe, stands Zeke.

"Oh, I didn't tell you to stop, just to skip all the drama and get to the point", he says, acting innocent.

"And what exactly is the point?" I ask, not even sure if I want to know the answer.

Zeke laughs dryly. "Oh, sweetheart, what do you think the point is?"

"I don't know", I spit, "that's why I asked."

Zeke's eyes turn darker at my words and Nick's warning about how the other guys are getting tired of me rings in my ear.

"Lay back with the attitude", Zeke says, "You're here because Nick wants you to. If you haven't heard it already; You belong to Nick, and you better start acting like it."

I cross my arms in front of my chest and give him a death stare.

"Or what?"

I'll admit that angering Zeke isn't the smartest thing to do but the way he acts makes me want to punch him in the face, hard.

Nick doesn't own me. He never had and never will.

Speaking of which, I can see Nick moving closer towards me from the corner of my eyes and I slowly back away again.

Zeke watches us as if we're the actors in a theater play.

"Nick, show her who's in charge."

I turn towards Nick, my eyes showing the confusion I feel and some of the fear I try to hide. Not being the slightest scared of them is plain stupid. They are maniacs and they kidnapped me and hurt my friends. Of course, I feel some fear.

Nick meets my gaze, moving his hand to caress my cheek. I flinch back but he takes a hold onto my hips and drags me back, forcing my body against his.

"Don't", he whispers in my ear, "you're being tested."

He starts nibbling on my earlobe and my confused face wrinkles into a face of disgust. The sound of Zeke chuckling makes my blood boil but I stay on my ground as Nick moves from my earlobe to my neck, leaving wet kisses on the way.

"Oh, cheer up, buttercup!" another voice suddenly speaks up and I only know one person who calls me that.

Kirk.

I groan in frustration but then I realize that they can take it as another sign, and I bite my lip to stop.

Nick's lips grace gently over my skin but as I can feel him finding my weak spot, I try to pull away and succeed with breaking the contact.

Behind me, I can hear comments and booing from Zeke and Kirk.

Nick moves one of his hands from my hip to my lower back and pulls me back, making the booing turn into cheering.

He roughly kisses me on my lips and pushes me up against the wall, forcing me to put my legs around him in order to not fall. I can feel rather than see him smirking into the kiss and as he licks my bottom lip asking for entrance.

I deny him access and a growling sound escapes his throat at my action.

"Kiss back!" Zeke shouts. I ignore him and focus on getting out of Nick's grip.

"Kiss him, or we'll pay Patricia another visit, or maybe even Lindsey?"

No.

Nick asks again.

I let him.

Our tongues fight for dominance, I lose, and almost gag in the progress.

Once again, I imagine kissing my ex, Shane, instead of Nick.

Just to make it bearable

My fingers pull through his hair with one hand and I hold onto the hem of his shirt with my other.

It feels like we go on forever before we get interrupted by a sudden lightning that disappears as fast as it comes, but I recognize it, and no one can miss the snapping sound that followed.

It was a camera flash.

Someone took a picture.

Both of our heads snap up and look in the direction of Zeke and Kirk. Both of them are holding a mobile in their hand with the camera pointed at us.

"Perfect", they say simultaneously and I can feel my cheek blush.

Not only did they see my full make-out session with Nick, but they took a picture of it too.

"Seriously?" I mutter, still stuck in the awkward position with my arms around Nick.

Nick doesn't seem to be bothered at all, more like the opposite.

"You send it to me, guys. Right?" At that, I hit him in the head with my palm and clear my throat to indicate that I want to get out of his grip.

"Ouch, what was that for?" he yells in a dramatic voice as he let my feet back down on the ground.

"For you being a jerk", I mutter.

Now when the make-out session is over, my old emotions flows back and overwhelms me.

"Is this how's it gonna be?" I ask in a strong voice, "me being here like a toy you can play with whenever you feel like it? Without any rights to do what I want?"

Nick and Zeke answer at the same time, but not with the same answer.

"Pretty much", Zeke says.

"Not really", Nick mumbles.

Kirk just stands there, glancing between me, Zeke and Nick.

"What?" I groan at him as he doesn't stop.

He meets my gaze and smiles, scratching the back of his neck in what I think is supposed to be a cute or hot gesture.

"Nothing", he smirks, "it's just that... if you're as good at kissing as it seems, I'll gladly take Nick's place sometime."

At that, Nick punch him playfully in the shoulder, not holding back on the force behind it.

Normally I would've at least rolled my eyes at their actions, but as I've already said; I'm not in the mood.

Patricia is stuck in this house, hurt and shielded from the outside world, thanks to me.

Lindsey, my best friend, is currently in the hospital for major injuries, thanks to me.

My life has gone from plain old normal and fine to a living hell, thanks to Nick.

I start thinking about the past I want to forget, thanks to Nick.

I've changed, thanks to Nick.

All of this is thanks to Nick.

It's all his fault.

Chapter 30: Unmasked

"Rise and shine, gorgeous." Someone shakes my shoulders, causing me to groan in dissatisfaction.

"Leave me alone", I mutter and I feel his chest vibrating as he chuckles.

My eyes widen in the speed of light as I realize I'm lying on top of him and I immediately shoot up from my place, his hand that shook me falling off of my shoulder in the progress.

"Someone suddenly got an energy kick", he says with amusement, "you know, you were quite adorable when you were sound asleep, cuddled up against my chest."

I make a gagging noise and pretend to stick two fingers down my throat.

"Please tell me you just lied."

He shakes his untidy hair and smirks.

"Nope. You even wrapped your arms around me, too bad you're not the same awake."

"Yeah", I sigh with my voice dripping with sarcasm, "too bad."

Still in my groggy morning state, I don't have time to comprehend his next action before it's too late and he's straddling me.

"Now, what have I said about that attitude? You need to lay it back", he says with a tone of both amusement and seriousness.

His eyes then flicker down to my lips with a lustful glint and I shake my head at him.

"No, seriously Nick. I'm not in the mood." I still - obviously- haven't gotten over what he did to Lindsey.

"But you broke one of the rules and you're attitude need to change, now. Lay it back", he repeats and leans in closer, kissing my lips harshly but not pinning my hands down my side or over my head.

That's it.

I'm done with his shit.

Before I really have time to think it through, I clench my hand into a fist and punch Nick right in his face, my knuckles hurting as I come in contact with his nose.

Nick let out a scream of pain and shoot back, his hands reaching up to his now bloody nose.

"What the hell?!" he shouts as I take the advantage and push him off of me and scurry into the bathroom, locking the door behind me.

"Alex!" he groans and starts banging at the door, but the banging soon stops and I hear the sound of a door slam shut, figuring he went to a nearby bathroom to get cleaned up.

I think about make a run for it, go through the door which I heard he didn't lock, and try to get out, but before I have time to put my plan into action I hear running footstep coming closer.

I recognize the voices as Zeke's and Vince's and I curse under my breath as my chance is ruined.

"Alex..." I hear Zeke say, "we know you're in there and you better come out now before you're getting yourself into serious trouble."

Like if I haven't already.

"Alex..." he repeats angrily, "open the damn door now or you'll regret it. You got a warning yesterday and now your free passes are gone. You better face reality, not hide from it."

But hiding is exactly what I want to.

My whole body freezes as I realize how much trouble I just gotten myself into.

Zeke's seriously pissed off and I got a feeling of that making him angry is one of the last things you want to do.

"If I get out now you'll hurt me anyway, so what's the point?" I call through the door, my voice trembling slightly.

"Yes", Zeke answers, "but we won't hurt you as badly."

I mentally roll my eyes at his 'soothing' words.

"Thanks, but no thanks", I reply, "I'm fine where I am."

Honestly, I'm really scared but I still don't regret punching Nick.

By all means, he deserved it.

"We're just going to break through the door if you don't open up",
Vince grunts.

"I'll take all the time I can get."

At least the words came from my heart. Finally being able to say what
I want, knowing I'm already in some serious trouble, feels amazing.
Except for the serious trouble part... but I take what I can get.

Suddenly another pair of footsteps comes into the room, but if I'm
not mistaken, I can also hear a quiet sobbing.

"Oh, Alex", Nick sings out in a mocking tone, sending chillers down
my spine, "you want to play a game?"

I don't reply, but listen to the sobs I'm now sure of is there.

Nick chuckles and continues as I don't make a sound.

"For every minute you stay in there, Patricia here will take a part of
your punishment. For every minute you are selfish enough to stay in
there and let your friend take the blame for you, she'll scream out in
pain."

It feels like a cold hand takes a firm grip around my heart and threat-
ens to crush it.

No.

A piercing scream then fills the tense air and the second later I literally slam the door open, causing it to hit the wall with a loud bang.

"L-leave her alone..." I stutter, trying to stay strong but failing.

Nick looks up at me, his eyes dark with anger and his facial expression tense.

"Gladly", he smirks and chuckles dryly, but it sounds more like a chalk being drawn against a chalkboard. Another unpleasant chiller sends down my spine.

He releases her from the painful grip he'd taken on her arm, and she falls to the ground with a whimpering sound and tears in her eyes.

"I'll handle it from here, guys", he tells Zeke and Vince who nods simultaneously and walks out of the room, after grabbing Patricia roughly by her sore arm and tugging her with.

As the door slam shut, Nick turns his head towards me.

Something seems to be off with him.

He doesn't look the same, the glimpse in his dark eyes isn't the same. Earlier, it was either a glimpse of amusement or lust but now, all I can see is fury.

I've never seen him like this.

His hair is messy and together with his clenched jaw and tense body, it makes him look like a maniac.

I gulp and stare him right in the eye, all sign of the old Nick gone.

Maybe this is the real him.

Chapter 31: Phobia

This chapter contains themes that some readers may find upsetting and/or disturbing due to water-related violence/abuse

It feels like the time slows down as I meet Nick's gaze. He doesn't look away and the glimpse in his eyes scares me and in the end, I'm the one who budges.

My eyes trail down his body as I breathe heavily, waiting for his first move.

The veins on his throat and neck are clearly visible and his hands are clenched into fists.

"You shouldn't have punched me, Alex", he says after countless of seconds in silence. I lower my lashes, look down at my feet, and bite my lip.

"I'm sorry...?" I whisper, but it comes out like a question and I glance up at him, starting to twinning my hair between my index- and middle finger.

"Sorry doesn't cut it this time", he tells me in an almost as quiet voice as me but the coldness in his tone scares me and as he takes a step towards me, a shiver runs down my spine and I take a step back.

"Then what can I do?" I try to plead without sounding too desperate, but all I get is a headshake.

"Nothing. That's how much you can do."

I open my mouth to literally beg him not to hurt me, but the words get stuck in my throat and I can't seem to utter them.

That's what he wants.

He wants me to beg him for mercy, he wants to feel like he's in total control and most important of it all; He wants to see with his own eyes that he's broken me.

I can't let that happen.

When Zeke left with Vince and Patricia, they slammed the door shut but they didn't lock it.

If I manage to get through the door I'll get a minimal chance of getting away. I can already tell for sure that the odds won't be in my favor, but it would postpone my punishment. And probably make it worse too, but I got to do this.

I can't just let Nick control me like a puppet.

"What will you do to me?" I ask Nick to buy time.

"You'll see", he sneers, "but firstly, do you got any phobias?"

My eyes widen slightly as I figure out his plan. Using my phobias against me. That's just pure evil and heartless. Only a monster would do that and that's just another proof of Nick's true nature.

I shake my head at his question.

"No, I don't. Except for one, and it's to be stuck with you forever."

He laughs dryly, the sound escaping his throat sounding more wicked and evil than if it would've come from the devil himself.

"Too bad you already have to face that fear and you better start enjoying it."

I pretend to gag at his words, realizing my mistake moments after as I see the anger flashing in his eyes.

"That's it. You've gotten too many chances. I didn't want it to come to this but the other guys are right. I've been too gentle with you but that's gonna change now with starting from your punishment. If you don't have any real phobia, I'll give you one."

With that, he throws himself at me and I move in the last second and sprint towards the door.

My hand reaches the handle and I'm just about to pull it down when I feel Nick taking a hold onto my hips, digging his fingers into the bone and causing me to whimper in pain.

I try to punch him and to kick him, I even try to bite him, but nothing works and I am grasping in the air for something to grab on to.

"Let me go!" I yell, not caring about the pointlessness in the action. Once the panic takes over, you don't control your actions like before.

"I hate you", tears of anger falls down my cheeks, "I hate you so much. You're a monster and I will never love you. Ever."

At the last words, I think I pushed too far because suddenly, I'm thrown against the wall and knock my head and back onto the hard concrete.

I groan in pain but before I manage to get up on my own, Nick takes a firm hold onto my upper arm and practically drags me into the bathroom.

My fear gets mixed with confusion as I see Nick tap up water in the sink and put the plug on. I try to wiggle out of the grip, bit it's in vain. Nick is too strong.

The grip is hurting me and I'm sure that it will leave bruises but that's the least of my worries right now.

The water fills the sink to the top and Nick smirks at me and I'm sure that I'm looking like a frightened deer. With his free hand, he takes a strong hold onto my hair and I scream in pain, but it ends up being muffled by the water I'm pressed into.

I start to panic even more as my lungs fills with water and I'm struggling to get over the surface with my hands - without succeeding.

I scream in the water for Nick to let me go, bubbles filled with air forming by my lips and floating to the surface.

Just as I start to feel light headed, I'm suddenly roughly pulled up and I immediately gasp for air.

"What do you think of your punishment?" Nick smirks, "I figured I didn't want to hurt the pretty face of yours."

He doesn't even give me time to reply before I'm pressed into the water again, but this time I manage to take a deep breath right before I hit the water, which is freezing cold for the record.

I hope that Nick will pull me back up to the surface soon enough before I run out of air, but I'm not that lucky. It seems like he knows exactly when the lack of oxygen is enough for me to pass out because it's not until then he pull me back up again. I gasp for air once again before getting my head pressed down - again. I don't even have time to take a full deep breath, but I am cut off halfway and swallow some of the water instead.

My lungs are screaming for air, my chest hurting, but Nick keeps going on.

And on... and on.

He continues with the procedure; pulling me down until my head is about to explode due to lack of oxygen, then pulling me up long enough for me to inhale quickly before pressing me down again.

Saying that I've got panic is an understatement.

I want to stay strong but as I'm in the water, helpless, it's hard.

I panic because every time I'm under the surface, I'm not pulled back up until right before I'm about to black out.

No matter how much I try not to, I'm fighting with my arms in vain because my brain tells me to.

Even though it's the last thing I want to do, I find myself begging Nick to stop.

He doesn't listen.

Nick's POV:

I ignore her pleadings and shove her back under the surface. Truth to be told, I'm not regretting what I'm doing.

This way, I won't hurt her that much physically but a lot more mentally. Physically, she'll be recovered in a matter of minutes but mentally on the other hand... it will leave her invisible scars.

If the only way to get her to listen to me is by scaring her, I'll do it.

All I want is for her to stay with me.

What's mine will stay mine.

What belongs to me will stay with me unless I say otherwise, which I don't do in this case.

Alex's mine and I want her to stay, therefore she will. No matter if she wants it or not.

A smirk is tugging at the corner of my lips as I see her futile attempt of getting out of the water and I wait for the right time, right before she'll pass out because of lack of oxygen, and pull her up.

Her eyes show fear as she looks at me with tears in her eyes and trembling lips. My smirk grows as she opens her mouth to beg me once more, and I shove her back in.

I continue with the action for countless of minutes until Alex's pointless attempts of getting free are long gone and she's given up and just sobs the short time she gets over the surface.

Her pitch black hair hangs in stripes around her cute face and I smile at her as she looks at me, completely terrified.

"You've learned your lesson?" I ask her as I'm towering over her.

Alex's POV:

I flinch back as he asks me the question and moves closer.

My shirt is soaking wet and my whole body is trembling, but not only by the cold.

When I stared into his eyes in the bedroom, right after when the other guys walked out, I thought that I could take the punishment, even though I was scared.

I was wrong.

If I would have gotten the chance to chose between the punishment I got, and being punched and kicked, I would have chosen the other alternative without any doubt.

I thought I was strong, but it seems like I've broke because of some water.

Only glancing at the water makes me shiver.

Never have I been so scared as I've been the last... countless of minutes that passed as I was slowly tortured in the water.

I knew he wouldn't kill me but that didn't stop the panic from rising inside of me.

It's an instinct. If you can't breathe, you'll fight for your life after the air you are in desperate need of.

It doesn't matter if you know that it will be fine moments after because the panic won't leave, and honestly, I don't think I'll ever forget the fear of being trapped under the icing cold water.

When Nick told me that he would give me a phobia since I didn't really have one, I thought he wouldn't succeed.

I wish I was right but sadly, I'm not.

I think I'm in shock because I barely notice and even less care when Nick picks me up and walk out of the bathroom and placing me on the bed.

He takes off his own shirt, which has gotten wet too, and slip under the covers with me, pulling my cold and tense body into his chest.

I can feel him stiffen behind me as he notice my cold shirt and he moves his hand to the hem of my shirt and starts tugging at it.

It's not until then I seem to care or show any emotions at all, but my hand immediately snaps to his and pulls down my shirt.

"C'mon, gorgeous..." he coos, "you're cold and you're in shock. It's not a good combination. You got to get the shirt off of you."

I don't reply and truth to be told, I barely hear him either. It's like I'm a mile away. His voice is just a sound in the background but I can't make out what he's saying and I can't concentrate on anything at all.

I'm just staring right in front of me, my body and mind absent.

It almost feels like a dream, unreal.

I can't take in what is happening, the only thing I can make out is the heat that is radiating off of Nick's hot body to my cold and still, thanks to the shirt, wet one.

Everything else is a blur.

Chapter 32: Numb

Alex's POV:

I wake up to numbness, realizing that I somehow fell asleep. My heart is beating in my chest, the blood is coursing through my veins and I breathe every now and then, but I feel... empty.

I barely even feel Nick's arms that are secured around my waist, let alone caring about it.

Nick is here, not even an inch away from me, but it still feels like I'm miles away.

I still feel absent, like if I'm dreaming.

Am I?

I don't know, it's like if I can't make out the lines in the outskirt of my eyes, it's a blur, but a little voice in the back of my head is telling me that it's reality. I don't listen.

I've never taken any drugs, but maybe this is how it feels to be high?

Normally I would've been frustrated because I can't even remember all of the yesterday's events, all my mind is making up as I think about it is a picture of water and a feeling of panic.

It felt like I drowned, but I didn't, I think.

Nick pulled me back up, but he also pulled me down.

Just thinking about him brings back the picture of water and feeling of panic, and I feel the fear and panic hitching up my throat, suffocating me.

My eyes start to water as the panic takes over, and my breathing gets heavier and quickens up a pace.

I grip the hem of the shirt I'm wearing, not noticing it's a different one than yesterday, and a whimpering sound escapes my lips and my body start to shake uncontrollably.

Nick's POV:

My arms are secured around her small body, my chest bare and my body heat radiating off to her.

I never left her side since she finally managed to fall asleep yesterday. I did change her shirt, though. I don't know if it's good to fall asleep once you're in shock or not, but she looked so peaceful that I didn't want to wake her up again, but the shirt's another story.

Yes, I did shake her up pretty badly, but I don't want her to get in such a bad state of shock that I can't reach her at all, but I think I might have failed at that part.

I suddenly feel her body stiffen and then start to shake uncontrollably as she whimpers. I sit up straight in the speed of light and start to roughly shake her by her shoulders.

"Alex!" I whisper-shout but raise my voice as she doesn't reply. "Alex! Alex, Alex, Alex!"

Still, no response. Just whimpering sounds and non-stop shaking.

I curse, worried and frustrated, and raise my hand and slap her on her cheek, hard.

She flinches at the pain and everything goes dead silent. She stops whimpering and shaking, and I sigh in relief, glad that it worked.

My legs are on either side of her waist and I lean in closer to her, resting my weight on one of my elbows, and lift up her chin and force her to look at me.

The icing blue eyes I meet almost look alien to me.

At first, I can't make out any feeling at all in her oh so beautiful eyes, but then I catch a glimpse of something that I know by far too well.

Fear.

"You don't have to be afraid of me", I whisper in her ear soothingly, "You haven't realized it yet, but I care for you, Alexandra", I say and uses her full name for a change. I leave a kiss on her forehead and mumble against her soft skin. "I care for you very much."

Unlike the normal Alex, I've learned to know and like, she doesn't move away or flinch the slightest. It's like she's turned off her emotions and I guess I should be happy for it.

"C'mon, we might as well get up since we're both awake anyway." I get off of her and walk to my closet and quickly change, it's not like she's watching me. Not that I mind if she would've.

"You coming?" I ask as I'm done and she still hasn't moved from her spot on the bed. It's like talking to a wall. She doesn't reply and I sigh heavily and scoop her up in my arms, carrying her out of my room bridal style.

I thought about changing her clothes but then turned town the thought as I figured it wouldn't be fair. I won't take advantage of her like that and especially not when she's still shocked and won't fight back the slightest.

I enter the kitchen and am welcomed by a strong smell of fried bacon.

"Someone seems to be in a happy mood", Zeke laughs from one of the barstools at the island, pointing at Alex with a mug of coffee.

I scoff in response and sit down on the stool on the opposite side of the island, placing my girl on my lap.

"Where's everyone else?" I ask as I look through the kitchen. No one else here.

"Getting ready", Zeke sneers, "I would've told you yesterday but you seemed to be too busy, but we've changed the plans a bit."

I furrow my eyebrows together. Today's the day we'll going to the black market to get rid of Aubrey.

"We're taking the girls with us", Zeke says and I tighten my grip on Alex.

"Why?"

Zeke chuckles quietly at my reaction.

"Relax, we won't sell her", he points at Alex again, "but we figured out that it would to them good to see what will happen if their parents don't pay and we don't want them anymore."

I roll my eyes, despite the serious in the situation.

"Tell me the real reason", I say with my jaw clenched, knowing that what Zeke just said can't be the only argument.

Zeke takes a sip of the coffee in his mug before answering.

"We don't trust Peter. As you know, the police have him under questioning and we don't know if he'd told them about this place. Leaving the girls here, it doesn't matter if someone's here to watch them or not, is a big risk. The police might as well be lurking in the bushes outside by now and waiting for the right time to strike when we have our guards down. You know it, Nick. We all know it."

I nod slowly. We've discussed this not long ago and we've been contemplating on whether or not we should move. We all voted on moving to our other house hours and hours from here, and we've decided to get out off here as soon as we've gotten rid of the girls, one way or another - which means through the ransom money or the black market.

We know for a fact that Peter can't have spilled the secret about the black market at least because we settled the date when he was no longer present.

Zeke empties the last in his cup and stands up. "We're leaving in an hour", he says before walking out of the room after putting the cup in the sink, hoping it would somehow wash itself.

I look at Alex, who is out of the window without focusing her eyes on anything particular.

Knowing I can't get her to eat anything, I empty the rest of the bacon that's left in the frying pan and fix myself something to eat. I'm not in the mood for forcing food down her throat.

I thought the hour I had left to kill would feel like an eternity, but the minutes passed by surprisingly fast and in what felt like no time, I stood in front of one of our cars, getting into the passenger seat with Alex still in my arms.

Luckily for me, Aubrey and the other girls sat in another car with Vince and Kirk. I don't think I would've been able to put up with her screams and cries.

Zeke starts the car which gives out a roaring sound before we roll down the road and out through the gates. I press my lips against Alex's cheek and rest my chin on top of her head.

Chapter 33: Market

Nick's POV:

We arrive at the black market and get out of the car. I still keep Alex in my arms and she still hasn't spoken. It's funny how Alex can be so damn quiet as the other girls -including Patricia- are screaming at the top of their lungs, but then, none of them are in shock.

Vince and Kirk step out from the other car, dragging the girls along and putting duct tape over Aubrey's mouth to keep her quiet. The other girls are just sobbing, but it seems like there's no off button to Aubrey's heartbreaking screams.

"Everyone ready to go?" Zeke asks and everyone nods and we start moving towards the gray industrial building where the market is held.

We reach the run down door in a matter of minutes and it squeaks loudly when we open it and walk through. Next up is a dark corridor, the only light of source coming from the one lamp attached to the wall which flickers and is on the verge to break.

By the next door, there's a heavily built guard watching it, and normally we would've said our names and reason for being here, but we're already well known here and the guard recognizes us since before.

He scoffs and mutters something we can't hear, before wiping off some sweat from his bald forehead and then putting in the code to the heavy door.

We don't say thanks, we're not known for being polite, and walk through the door.

A strong smell of cigarettes immediately hit us and the air is thick with smoke. Zeke brings out a cigarette himself and lit it. He holds out the package for me to take, but I shake my head.

We walk to the back of the room and pass both young and old men on the way. There are a few girls here too, but barely anyone except for the ones that are up on the market.

I sit down on a crimson red sofa and pull my feet up at the table in front of it, gently placing Alex in a comfortable position on my lap, her head resting against my shoulder. Her body is tensed and her lips slightly parted, like if she's about to say something, but she doesn't.

Zeke sits down beside me, I feel the cushions sink down a bit under his weight, and Danny sits on a wooden chair by the table that's now working as my footrest.

The other guys disappeared somewhere, some of them to go behind the stage with Aubrey, and some of them to probably meet old acquaintances or buy something to drink.

Whatever they did, they came back within a few minutes, except for Kirk who stayed with Aubrey.

"Here you go", Vince says and hands me a beer. He didn't ask me if I wanted it because he already knew I would.

"She's still not answering, huh?" he then says and eyes Alex. I sadly shake my head and open the can and take a sip of what's inside.

"No, she's not. Didn't think it would affect her so much."

"What did you even do?" he asks and I realize I haven't told anyone and I grin.

"Just gave her a little water to bath her pretty little head in."

Vince chuckles slightly and take a sip of his own beer before sitting down on the free side next to me.

I sigh and lay back my head and close my eyes for a moment. A small headache has formed in my temple and I pinch the bridge of my nose with my free hand.

After a couple of seconds, I open my eyes again and they immediately adjust to the dull light. My hand moves from my face down to Alex's thigh as my eyes travel over the people in the room. Some, most, of the faces are familiar, but it's also some new ones I don't recall that I've seen before. Like the man in a black suit near the exit. He wears a white shirt underneath the black blazer, and it seems to be too neatly fixed compared to everyone else's clothing. Same thing goes for his hair. It's light and pretty messed up, but it seems like he tried too much. Like if he tried to make it look messy on purpose without indicating that he'd put any effort in styling it, but his original haircut gives it away. It's too neatly cut, not layered or damaged at all. It wouldn't even be a little bit out of place if it wasn't for the styling product he'd put in. Maybe it just looks like that, or maybe he's vain. Not that it matters for me at all.

What does catch my attention, on the other hand, is his eyes that seem to flicker through the room over and over again, and when it lands on the corner where we are, he immediately look away like if he'd been caught doing something he shouldn't. I watch him intensely, not even caring to hide my stare. I think it makes him uncomfortable because I can see his Adam's apple move as he gulps and look away towards the stage.

If there's something about a place like this, a black market, it's to not trust nor upset anyone. It might not end very pretty.

The light suddenly flickers and then goes off completely, the room bathing in darkness a few seconds before the light by the stage goes on again, this time even lighter than before.

A man in his late thirties comes forward, holding a microphone in his hand, and introduce himself. I already know who it is since I've been here more than once and he's been the host the latest years ever since the host before him got busted by the cops.

If you're into the illegal business, nothing's safe, but you sure as hell can make a lot of money.

The man on the stage, known as Ty, explain how the bidding will work - if there by a chance is any newcomers here who don't know about it - and then it starts.

First up is some drugs and I lost my interest halfway through the bidding. We're not here to sell or buy drugs, we just want the money for Aubrey and then we'll leave.

I notice that the man in a neat suit is talking on his phone, and I caught him glancing over at our table once again.

My eyebrow furrows together. What's his problem?

I take another look at him, suspicious about his true identity, and then notice that he takes eye contact with someone across the room.

I follow his gaze that lands on a middle-aged man with short, brown hair and a mustache. The man with a mustache glances over at me and that's when I get the hint that something really isn't as it should.

I elbow Zeke in his ribcage and he almost chokes on his cigarette and gives me a glare, but the glare vanish as he sees my serious face.

"Wha-", he starts but gets cut off by Ty who practically shouts into the microphone to get everyone's attention.

Ty calls up the next one on the stage, and Aubrey stands up, but she's not the only one.

From the corner of my eyes, I see someone from underneath the stage stand up as well.

"Everyone freeze!", the one who stood up says, holding a gun in his two hands. It's the neatly dressed man. "Hands up in the air where we can see them. We're from the police." I notice that the man with the mustache is standing up as well, along with yet two other ones. They are all armed with a gun and I hear Vince curse behind me.

"Shit."

I agree.

Chapter 39: Lost And Won

Alex's POV:

A gunshot goes off and chaos breaks loose. People scream and shout, out of fear or to each other, and running bodies fills the room.

I, on the other hand, barely notice anything at all and am almost thrown at the floor as Nick abruptly rises from his place on the sofa, but he catches me in the last second before I would practically faceplant the floor.

He tries to desperately drag me towards one of the exits, but I'm still numb and he curses in frustration as I move as much as a dead body. With other words, I don't move at all.

Zeke and the other guys are out of sight, somewhere in the sea of panicking bodies, and everyone moves towards the two exits, pressing against each other like if their lives depends on it - which it might as well do.

Nick pulls out a gun from the hem of his jeans, hid behind is back and shirt, and suddenly I'm pushed by my side - hard - by a creepy looking guy who runs past, probably not even noticing me. I, however, fall to the ground by the strength behind the push, bringing Nick down with me.

If I would think rationally - normally - I would've thought that Nick would get both of us up as soon as possible but instead, he throws himself over me to keep me down on the ground. Not that I would've moved anyway.

A bullet flies past me, over my head, and Nick's action makes total sense.

He aims his own gun and fire but I don't know if he hit something or not, I'm still in my own little world far, far away from what's going on.

Far far away from the chaos, and Nick's tense body that's pressed against mine.

What I don't know, is that most of the people who runs through the exit don't make it outside, because except from the four policemen inside, more and even more of them are guiding all doors and windows, and they keep coming, the sound of the sirens becoming mixed with the screams, shouts, and gunshots.

"Alex", Nick whispers-shouts in my ear even though I can't hear him, his breath panting, "you have to come back."

He's still on top of me, and he takes a firm grip on my chin and forces me to look at him.

"Alex, please. Come back, I don't care about how stubborn and angry you are. Heck, I don't even care about the fact that you hate me, not right now. All I want is for both of us to get out of here alive, and I can't do it without your help." His dark eyes, now full of worry, stress and nervousness, looks into mine, searching for some kind of proof that I'm here, back. He doesn't find any and neither do I find back to reality.

Nick starts to get desperate, knowing he can't carry me out of here, not if he wants us to be the slightest bit safe at least, and his lips attacks mine. He kisses me harshly, his lips moving against my numb ones, hoping for a miracle that will bring me back. Sadly, things like that only happen in fairy tales and movies and I can guarantee that I'm not the sleeping beauty and that Nick isn't prince Philip.

A tear, yes a tear, falls down Nick's cheek and lands on my chin. If it's caused out of frustration or sadness, I don't know.

"Damn it, Alex!" He curses as he pulls back, gun in hand.

The man, cop, with a mustache stands across the room and his eyes flicker through the room, finding Nick and me.

His hands, steadily placed on a gun, points at us, or more directly, at Nick.

"Leave the girl!" he shouts as he cautiously makes his way towards us, keeping an eye on everyone around as well, watching out for any gun pointed at him.

Apparently, he's not cautious enough and with most of his focus pointed at Nick and the gun Nick is holding, the policeman doesn't see Zeke who's standing a couple meters behind him, covered behind a panel by the scene. A glimpse of silver glistens in the light of one of the lamps above the scene and without anyone really noticing, Zeke pulls the trigger on the gun in his hand and it fires, the policeman falling to the ground with his eyes widened in surprise and shock. The bullet didn't hit him in the head or heart and the policeman drops the gun, not being able to hold it as pain is shooting through his whole body from his left side where a dark liquid starts pouring out.

"Nick, get your ass over here!" Zeke shouts.

"Alex won't move", he shouts back and Zeke curses loudly and turned his head side to side, checking his surroundings.

"Cover me", he yells over all the muffled screams before throwing himself into the sea of bodies, hoping he won't get shot.

The policemen at the east exit have fallen because of all the pressure from all the pushing people who fought for their lives to get out, and more and more people leaked out of the building. Some of the people weren't that lucky and are now lying on the floor, either because of a gunshot or because they fell under the pressure. However, the people on the ground has all luck against them and are stamped and kicked on by criminals who probably doesn't even know that the poor souls on the ground are there.

Zeke makes his way to Nick and me without getting hurt.

"Let's get out of here", he says, panting with sweat glistening on his forehead.

Nick nods and moistens his lips. The room is hot, too hot, and the air is full of smoke.

Too much smoke...

Nick's nostrils fill with the sticking smell of the smoke, but it doesn't smell like cigarettes, no it smells like real fire like something is burning.

With a nagging feeling in his stomach, Nick turns his head 180 degrees and is met by the sight of orange flames, not big ones, but still.

One of the many cigarettes in the room has caught fire to a few thrown away magazines, which have spread the fire to the nearby sofa.

The flames aren't that big, not yet, but it's only a matter of minutes before the smoke and heat become deadly.

Zeke and Nick takes a firm grip around my upper arms and forces my body up, throwing my arms over their shoulders before walking towards the east exit.

It's a miracle neither of them has gotten shot but I guess the police prefer talking with a big mouth then taking action. No one, except for these psychopaths that are holding me up and the criminals who are gathered here today, would enjoy shooting someone and even though I'm almost sure of that all of the criminals here aren't exactly best friends with each other, they would probably prefer getting away from the police than staying to kill one and another.

As we are close to the exit, we stop abruptly as the criminals who were pushing each other to get out, starts backing into the room again.

Nick and Zeke furrow their eyebrows in confusion before men, all dressed in blue, burst through the opening. Let's just say that there aren't just a few of them.

"Shit", they both say in unison.

The police are now overpowering the criminals by numbers, and the criminals in the room have realized it.

"Drop your guns!" a police officer shouts, like if he would be heard unlike the one before.

Instead of everyone dropping their guns, the effect get's the reversed.

Everyone starts shooting. Including the police.

We duck under one of the sofas, hiding from the gunshots, trying to keep out of the fight.

It's dark where we are, the lights - some of them trashed, shattered, because of gunshots - doesn't reach this far.

The smoke, on the other hand, will soon start forcing all of the people out of the building, where loads and loads of cops surely will be waiting.

"Where are the other guys?" Nick mutters, more to himself than to us, but Zeke answers anyway, his face suddenly tensing up and going a shade paler.

"There." He nods towards the scene, where Kirk, Will, and Danny stands with their hands behind their back, handcuffed by three cops who stands by their side.

I catch a glimpse of a familiar face moving towards the exit in a fast pace, accompanied by a man in blue.

It's Aubrey, and behind her, I recognize Nicole and Amy.

Crap, there's one girl missing.

The gunshots have toned down, the cops finally getting the upper hand, and no one stops the girls from slipping through the exit with the police officer.

A piercing scream is suddenly heard through all the other sounds, that now mostly comes from angry criminals who are busted and handcuffed.

As Nick and Zeke turn their head in the direction of the scream, they found Patricia in the arms of Vince, a gun pressed against her temple and two cops pointing their guns at both of them. Vince is shielding himself with Patricia's body, in case the cops would shoot.

"Hands up and let the girl go", one of the cops tells Vince in a raised voice.

Vince gives out a cold chuckle.

"You really think I'm that stupid?" he spits on the ground, "No. I won't let her go until you let me walk out of here freely."

Patria's eyes are full of tears, a few of them falling down her cheek.

"P-please don't do this..." she whimpers, directing her words at Vince.

He shakes his head in a no.

Something with her scream caught my attention, and something with hearing her whimper touched my heart.

It's not like it normally wouldn't, but since the shock settled in, I haven't cared or noticed anything.

Until now.

Vince pressed the barrel of the gun even harder against her temple, causing her to whimper out of fear again.

"Patricia..." I whisper, my voice raspy after not being used for a while. Both Nick and Zeke turns their attention towards me, eyes widened in surprise.

I ignore them and call for Patricia again, this time with a high voice.

"Patric-"

A hand covers my mouth before I have time to finish my sentence and I try to pin the hand off of me.

"Are you crazy?"" Nick says through gritted teeth. He's the one holding me. "The cops could have heard you!"

"They did", Zeke says slowly and takes a firm grip on the handle of the gun. Nick does the same and removes the hand from my mouth, leaning in closer to whisper in my ear.

"One second. You're back in one second and already screw up."

"I'm back in one second", I say, repeating his own words, "and I've already done something useful."

I turn my attention towards the cop who is slowly walking towards us.

"Be careful!" I warn her, "they got guns."

"A-allie?" Patricia stutters and I answer her immediately.

"Yes, Patricia?"

Nick gives me a glare, but quickly turn his head towards the cop in front of us. She is slowly moving towards us, her gun pointed in our direction, at Zeke to be exact.

"A-am I..." Patricia stars and my heart drop down my stomach as I realize where she's going, "Am I going to d-"

She's cut off by the sound of an explosion, and all of us in the room falls down to the ground.

The fire just got in contact with the stack of alcohol hidden behind the stage, and the small explosion it caused sat fire to some of the furniture that once was safe from the fire and now have turned into a part of it.

Smoke, more than ever before, fills the air and I cough and shield my eyes.

Someone, I don't recognize the voice, tells everybody to move out, exit the building, and I am quick to jump up from my place and run towards the door, but someone grip my arm and pulls me back.

"Not so fast, gorgeous" Nick sneers. "I've just got you back, which means I won't let you go again."

I know exactly what he means, even though he still technically had me as I was gone, but I don't have time to correct him. I fight against his grip but it won't loosen and I start to feel the panic creep up my throat.

"Nick, please", I say without making my voice sound pleading, "we have to get out of here now, otherwise we'll die of the smoke or fire."

"There's another exit behind the bigger flames which no one is watching, c'mon."

I know exactly which exit he means, it's the one we walked in through, and I also understand why no cops are guiding it, at least not from the inside. It's where the fire is at its highest, trying to get through the flames is pure madness.

Nick start to drag me there, even though I'm struggling to get out of his grip, and Zeke is already on his way.

"We can't leave Patricia!" I yell, searching around the room for her with my eyes. It's useless. The smoke is too thick and if I can't see her, it means she can't see me either, and neither can the police.

We're getting closer to the big flames, following the wall, and the heat is almost burning my skin and I cough once again, my eyes watering.

I trip at something by my feet and fall to the ground, once again dragging Nick down with me.

"We can't go in there!" I yell at him, "It's madness, suicide!"

"We can!" he shouts back, "I won't lose you again, let's go!"

He stands up again but I crawl backward and shake my head.

"No, Nick. It's over. You've lost."

I think he's looking at me in confusion but I'm not sure, the smoke is making my eyesight blurry.

"What do you mean?" he asks and I take a firm grip on the small object in my hands that I accidentally tripped over, trying to place my hands in the right position.

"I mean that it's all over", I say and cough a little, "I won the bet. I stepped out of the house without being broken. I'm out of the freaking hellhole, and I'm not scattered into a million pieces. And with that said, I'm done with you."

I raise the object in my hand with an uncomfortable feeling in my stomach as I feel the weight in my hand, but I can't back down.

"Alex, I-", Nick starts but he's cut off by me.

I pull the trigger on the gun in my hand, the gun I found as I fell, and the sound of the gunshot ring in my ears.

Nick screams in pain and I figure the bullet hit him but I don't walk to him to check. Instead, I drop the gun and run towards the east exit; towards safety.

Chapter 35: Free

A police officer meet me as I run outside the burning building and I search for Patricia and the other girls with my eyes, glossy because of the smoke, but the officer practically pushes me towards some paramedics who put an oxygen mask onto my face.

I take deep breaths, breathing on the air free of smoke, but I can't seem to stay still.

I have to know if Patricia and the other girls are alright, but even though the chaos in my though another ones slips in.

Nick.

I shot him. I never thought I had it in me, to aim and fire a gun at someone, but I guess being kidnapped changed that.

Being kidnapped changed me.

What if I killed him? All I wanted was to get away from him, not for him to die.

I'm not a killer, am I?

A tear falls down my cheek and it's not because of the smoke.

I breathe in again, filling my sooty lungs with pure air, welcoming it as it makes its way down my throat before my body forces me to breathe out again. I keep doing that over and over again, letting the good in and the bad leave my lips for the last time, until a paramedic takes it off of me after a few minutes.

I start to walk towards the direction of a crowd, but a policeman places a hand on my shoulders to stop me.

"Are you one of the missing students from Beckwith High School?" he asks in a tone I think is supposed to be gentle, but the tone reminds me of coarse sandpaper.

"Y-yeah", I answer and curse myself for stuttering, "I'm Alex."

He gives me a small smile that shows some wrinkles by his eyes.

"Alexandra, I assume", he says and I force a smile onto my lips as a reply.

"I'm officer Gordon and I've been following the kidnapping since the start."

I don't know what he wants me to answer. Something with 'Oh really, how was it?' It just seems stupid and I don't even want to know the answer. Instead, I start playing with a strand of my hair without noticing it.

"How did you find us?" I ask eventually as we fall into an awkward silence.

Gordon gives me another smile and motion for me to walk with him to an ambulance not too far away. I realize I don't even know if it's his first or last name. I think it's his last name, but I'm not sure.

"We wouldn't be here today if it wasn't for two of your friends, actually", Gordon says as we walk and he continues, "let's just say it was thanks to some cleverness from your friends and today's technology."

I don't question what he means because I figure out I will be getting the details later but now, I got a feeling of that Gordon wants me to be checked by the ambulance for any injuries.

I'm right.

He motions for me to go the last few steps to the paramedics on my own, and I do.

"They are just going to do a basic check-up on you", he tells me, "it's nothing to worry about."

I suck on the inside of my cheeks and nod, letting one of the paramedics direct me towards the back of the ambulance where the check-ups are held.

The girl who checks me tries to make some small talk but my mind is elsewhere and I can't concentrate on what she's saying. Eventually, she gives up and continues in silence. When she's done, she flashes me a smile and tells me everything's fine and I quickly walk away, feeling rather than hearing that Gordon follows me.

"Where are my friends?" I ask him without turning around to face him.

He waits a few seconds before answering and I think that he might have nodded in their direction but then realized that I didn't watch him.

"They are by the police cars to your left."

I turn my head in the direction he told me to, and at first, I can't see anything except for all the cops dressed in blue, but then I make out Patricia's blonde hair in the sea of people and my feet pick up the pace.

I press myself through the crowd and meet Patricia's green eyes in barely a second before we both engulfed in a hug.

"You're safe", I hear her whisper and hold me even tighter and I nod weakly.

"You too." My voice sounds weak as well, exhausted, and it's like all my energy suddenly washes off of me.

All the other girls - Amy, Nicole, and Aubrey - stands beside Patricia, looking slightly shocked. I can't blame them because I already have a hard time to believe, accept, that I'm out of that hellhole of a house.

I'm finally free.

Someone clears their throat and ruins the moment, disturbs my thoughts.

"We need to take you girls down to the station for questioning and then you can finally go home."

I saw something lit up in the eyes of the girls but instead of lighting up like them, it felt like something came crashing down and took my good mood away with it.

At least they got a family to go back to.

What about me? Will I go back to my old foster care with Carol, Brian, and Lottie? Or will my real parents, who finally seem to notice my existence, welcome me home once and for all?

Chapter 36: Reunion

Alex's POV:

After the questioning at the police station, I slowly walk out of the questioning room, dreading what's waiting for me on the other side of the door.

All the girls have walked ahead, thrilled and not even able to hide their excitement. All of them have family members who managed to get here by now.

Stopping by the doorframe, I take a deep breath before finally stepping out, my eyes glued to the floor as I do so.

A light voice, lighter than any other I've ever heard, shrieks in joy and I feel small arms wrap around me and I look down with a smile playing on my lips.

"Hello to you too, Lottie", I say to the ten years old hugging me, and I gently place my arms around her small body and hug her back.

"Alex!" she screams again, "you're back!"

I gulp, trying not to cry, and finally look up.

I expect to see only Carol and Brian, but there are two other adults there who aren't hugging or participating in any other family re-union. I recognize them from the news, it's my biological parents.

Carol and Brian, my foster parents, step forward from their seats by the door and hug me as well, still with Lottie holding onto my waist for dear life.

Carol keep telling me about how everything will be okay from now on and about how worried they've been and how glad they are that I'm back and as she finally seems to get it all off of her chest, she and Brian pull out of the embrace.

I meet the grey eyes of my mother, my biological mother, and feel Lottie releasing her grip on me.

I don't know if I'm supposed to be happy or mad.

Yes, my biological parents are finally here to see me, their daughter, but they did leave me in the first place. They are my parents, but they are also the reason to why I've never found a place I can call home.

Is it just to forgive and forget? Can it really be that easy?

I don't know, but it suddenly feels like it doesn't matter either.

The child in me takes over. The lost child who has been longing for a parent.

My vision becomes blurry because of tears that fill my eyes and falls down my cheek. I don't care about wiping them away, I can't seem to stop looking at the two strangers in front of me, the two strangers who should be one of the ones I'm closest to.

"M-mom?" I hear myself say in a voice barely above a whisper. I think she starts to cry too but I'm not completely sure, my vision is too blurry, but as I take a step towards her she does the same.

Her arms are thrown around me, pulling me into her warm embrace. I put my arms around her as well and welcome the other body that joins us, my dad.

I stayed in the embrace for what felt like forever before I finally pulled away and got a closer look at my parents. I got my mother's figure and hair, and my father's icing blue eyes.

Whose personality I've taken most from is left for me to find out.

I'm in a moment of bliss until an officer, Gordon to be exact, interrupts us with a frown on his face and a cup of coffee in his hand.

"I don't really know any good way to put this", he says honestly and his eyes graze over the room. All of us girls are still here and Gordon has caught our attention to the fullest.

"Well, uhm", he clears his throat, "we arrested three of the guys but three got away."

I feel my heart drop down my stomach.

"Which three?" I whisper, my hand gripping onto Carol's upper arm. Gordon shakes his head and gives me a sad look. "I'm sorry, Alexandra, but it was... let's see if I remember them right now... Zach? No, Zeke, Vincent and Nick."

"No." It feels like the temperature dropped as well and I start to cry again, but this time it isn't tears of joy.

"No, no, no..."

Arms wrap around me, belonging to more than just one, and I let myself get comforted by them as I quietly sob for a while before I get myself together and angrily wipe a tear away from my cheek with the back of my hand.

"I shot him", I say even though I already told that to the police during the questioning - I got away since it was in self-defense. "I shot him and I don't know where the bullet hit, but I know it did. He may not survive and even if he did, he wouldn't come back, right?"

Gordon shakes his head. "I'm sorry but I can't answer that question but it's highly unlikely that they would show up in the next few days and I highly suggest you all get home and rest. Let's take care of this tomorrow, one day at the time."

I decide to follow his advice.

This moment is special, and I won't let Nick ruin it. Somehow, the police will fix the problem, they have to.

Pushing all the worries away, I return to the moment of joy.

Lindsey joined us later on, not a second too late though, and together we all went to a nearby café. I felt exhausted but I couldn't sleep, not yet.

I had a lot to catch up on and as we entered the café and I ordered a cappuccino, all thoughts about sleep disappeared. No one talked about Nick either, which I was grateful for.

I enjoyed the feeling I got, sitting there in the booth with some of the most important people in my life. It felt nice, normal.

It was all I ever wanted.

I don't need fame to feel special - because I have people that love me at home.

Taking a sip of my cappuccino, I return to reality and the conversation my two pairs of parents are holding.

Everything is nice, cozy and simply perfect until we leave the booth and step out of the café.

Everyone goes ahead of me as I walk in the opposite direction to throw my now empty mug of cappuccino, I drank the last of it as we walked out of the door, and just as I throw it in the trash bin, I see movement by the corner of the building.

Blonde hair, tucked under a hood, and hands in the front pocket of the washed out jeans.

A tingling sensation spreads from my heart out to my fingertips, fear, and I blink and look at the corner again.

Nothing.

Did I just imagine it?

Shaking my head, I walk towards the corner as fear holds me in a stranglehold.

I half expect someone to pop up right in front of me as I peek around the corner of the building, and I half expect to see the back of a jacket disappear further into the darkness.

The street is completely empty and dead silent. No movement at all, no back disappearing further away from me.

Once again, I shake my head and tell myself I'm being paranoid.

It couldn't have been Zeke, right? He wouldn't show up here and then just leave again, would he?

Honestly, I don't know and therefore I keep telling myself I'm just being paranoid, but if that's the case, then why do I feel my nostrils stick by the smell of smoke?

Paranoia, I tell myself before heading back to the others, to my loved ones.

I can't ask for anything else because now, I have everything I need.

A smile, as pure as driven snow, makes its way onto my lips.

.

Milton Keynes UK
Ingram Content Group UK Ltd.
UKHW022126251124
451529UK00012B/712

9 781787 993945